Child of the Elements

Michael A. Susko

AllrOneofUs Publishing
Baltimore, Md & Huntsville, Al

While every precaution has been taken in the preparation of this book, the publisher assumes no responsibility for errors or omissions, or for damages resulting from the use of the information contained herein.

CHILD OF THE ELEMENTS

First edition. November 24, 2019.

Copyright © 2019 Michael A. Susko.

ISBN: 978-1393263647

Written by Michael A. Susko.

To my nephew Matt and his son Daxton.

To the Indigo children of the world.

And thanks to NovOntos for the use of his graphic, "Emerging Leaves" on the book cover.

PART I
CHAPTER I

Child of the Boughs

"Put him out in the field and let him die." She could still see the gesture, the hand cutting down like it was a sharp-edge stone. "Are you not small enough?"

Clutching her baby fiercely, Small One said nothing. When there was danger before, she could flee, but now she had the baby. Still, they would have to fight her, and her eyes looked wild. The two males backed down. One could have killed her easily enough, but they chose not to fight a mother.

"She is a Wild Child herself," one said.

"Her child will die anyway," said the other. "It's the way of things."

The young mother backed away and climbed into a tree, her night home. There she trembled, her woven grass skirt shaking. She calmed, then went down and set up sharp sticks around the tree's base, using half-sticks left by Sharpener. He was not around now. The sticks did not work so well against her own kind. She would have to stay up late and be prepared if they returned.

She wondered about Sharpener. Should she have put her hopes in him? She once had asked an old woman, who said, "Sharpener is a man of few words, but he does good deeds. Still, it is his nature to roam." Small One had decided that this was good enough, and she kept her heart with him.

The boy baby had been born early, unable to cling. "You know what happens with that type; they will soon die," a woman had warned her. "Why risk your life? You will be out in the field—yes, you are fast, but the leopard will race—and you won't be able to run to safety. You will have to let go of your baby to escape."

Small One only gripped her child tighter. She had learned to climb trees with her child in hand and place him in boughs. At times, she would leave the baby while she tended to things on the ground.

Small One was a trapper of birds, setting delicate snares. Her traps were good and caught many. She would not always kill what she caught. She would care for birds who were sick or injured, and they would become her friends. They did not fear being near her, and some even bedded near her night nest. Usually, one or two followed her into the fields. *Birds are my food and yet they have become my friends,* she wondered.

The others laughed at this foolishness, as a little bird meat did not interest them. "She is but a child herself," they said, "with one too young to be called a child." The men might have killed such an infant, but they had not.

Sharpener was a major reason, for he was her friend. Maybe Sharpener would protect her if the time came. Then again, he would be gone for days and might not be there when she needed him.

The mother knew her baby was not yet a full child, as he was much smaller and more helpless than others. Only his head was large. "He is one of us!" she had protested. The women believed her, but the men shook their heads and did not accept him.

The child was different in other ways. As he got bigger, he seemed to know the meaning of sounds quicker and make new ones.

When the men overheard him, they asked, "What words have you given him? How can he be one of us?"

"I know what he is saying," his mother defended. 'Your milk is sweet. The day is bright. I see green.'"

They laughed, but some were not sure. "Can a strange thing be good?"

"He is my baby. I did not find him," she answered firmly. That meant she would fight for his life. The doubters, for now, had largely let her be.

She held him apart, the baby babbling long strings of sounds. "Yes, my baby is not like the others. But he must live!"

Small One knew her child was special, and she held a secret she had told no one. On the third day after he was born, he uttered a new word. It sounded like *Manwey*. Could that be his secret name? she wondered? But a child does not name itself, so it must mean something else. Could it be a power that would protect him?

The early child, however, helped the mother gain a name. Because she made cradles of tree limbs for her baby, some called her *Bough*. Before, it had been *Small One*, or *Half-stick* for her use of broken spears, and sometimes *Wild Child*. Yet another name was *Trembling One*, for she would tremble when the world seemed so much bigger than her.

It happened as the woman had warned. Bough was out in the field with her child, for she needed to find a plant for her child's sickness and use a spring to cool its fever. A bird had followed her like one sometimes did.

A great spotted leopard had appeared and started circling. *The leopard comes at night, but here is one in the middle of the day!* She threw rocks, screamed, and held up her stick. The great cat, three times her size, was not deterred. The leopard's circle tightened. She spied larger rocks—she could run fast and hide in a small opening. But she could not make it with her baby. She backed away slowly.

Small One walked, laden with the child in her arms, and the leopard took it for weakness. As she moved toward the rocks, the leopard approached more directly. *The leopard will kill me before I can reach safety. I must think of something else.*

But Bough did not know what to do. She could not leave the child behind, and there were no stones to throw. There wasn't anything to do but to raise her stick and keep backing away.

Acting as if wounded, her bird friend tried to distract the leopard. The cat snapped at the bird, then ignored it. The leopard was impatient; his eyes flashed. Bough, with all her will, fought off the impulse to flee.

Suddenly, a pack of wolves appeared. The leopard startled, then turned and left. *I'm saved from the leopard, but I am left to wolves!* The pack paused, considered her. The wolves were not hungry, and Bough made no movement to provoke them. She did her best to show no fear, crossing her arms and holding her stick firmly with her baby behind her.

The lead wolf threw a long look her way and did not sense fear. He had encountered humans before and knew that sticks could cause wounds. But in the end, the wolves were not hungry, and they moved on. Two wolves lingered, but the lead wolf yapped his command.

After they passed, Bough collapsed, her trembling released. *It was luck; it was chance the wolves had come!* She had used all her strength to stand without shaking. Her bird friend came by her side, but she was too weak to get up.

The sun was setting when Sharpener found her, still faintly trembling. "Why are you laying here?" he demanded to know. "Do you not know the dangers of an open field?" He cast his gaze about and saw the leopard and wolf tracks. He wondered how she had survived, then answered an unasked question. "I saw your bird. He came back without you. Your child was not in the tree."

Small One summoned her strength and sat up, smiling. He had called her baby a child, the first male to do so.

Sharpener saw the smile. "Yes, I know you made him a Child. I know too, that he is a *New One*. Where did you find him?"

He knew the baby was hers, but he said this to distract her from trembling.

"It came from me!" Bough protested, and she stood up with a sudden fierceness. "Yet, I know he is not just from me."

"Who then?" asked Sharpener. "From the clouds? One of your bird friends?"

Bough did not answer. This was the most of late that Sharpener had talked to her, and one of the few times he teased her. She sensed Sharpener knew more. He was the only man who had been with her, so maybe he worked this magic.

But even if the child came just from herself, Bough knew she needed protection from a male. Sharpener was the only one who visited her with kindness. She held out the baby for him to hold, but he refused, putting his hand out. Yet when the baby reached out for him, he accepted him for a brief time. *Yes, he has held the baby,* she thought. *He has claimed it as his! No one will bother us now.* But Sharpener will still roam, and how long he will stay away she did not know.

The time came sooner than she feared. For two full moons, Sharpener was gone, and she realized that he might never come back. It seemed something must have happened, and what little protection she had for the baby was gone. The other men called her Small One again, and she sensed a male would soon try to claim her. What could be done? For the first thing the man would do would be to toss her child out of the tree.

Bough hid as much as she could, spending time in her tree home, trying to think of an answer. There was none. Her best hope was the return of Sharpener. *He will not stay away much longer,* she thought. *Did he not go into the field to find me when he saw my bird? Did he not call my baby a child? And did he not hold him? He will come back to him.* But she feared he could be dead. Despite his strength and sharpened stick, a wild animal could have killed him. Or worse, he could have run into a band of Fierce Ones.... Bough trembled and sobbed.

Her baby was a child, although still unnamed. If only Sharpener had given him a name, she could have used it before the others. The baby cried, not a full cry, and moved his head to the side. She fed him. "What is your name?" she asked. "You said a new word soon after you were born. Is Manwey your name, or will it be another new word?"

Bough decided she must give a name to the child herself. Yet, she could not think of one that would truly fit the child. *His name will come in time,* she thought. *For now, he is an Early Child. But that must remain hidden, for it does not show strength.* She must discover a name to share with others, lest they think less of getting rid of an unnamed one.

The taunts became worse, and Small One sensed that not even a name could save the child. There was another thing she could do. She could flee with the child. But to leave the group and be on her own would likely be death.

A man named White Hair, the oldest among them, sensed something. He had seen much and knew things before they happened. Bough had not gone to him for help, for he was too old to protect her. This time, he came to her.

"Things have changed for you," he began.

How does he know? she wondered. She had said nothing.

White Hair asked to see her child and placed his hand on his head. "Know this is a *New One.* Your best hope is to find others with ones like him. The baby must find his own kind, for in time, he will die if he stays here. Go east, toward the morning sun. Wolf People with *New Ones* are that way."

"What is a *New One*?" she asked, starting to tremble.

"What can I say? They are different and they are the same. They begin weak and become strong in a new way. I have seen others like them, but most have died. Sometimes, they are left on the Offering Hill; sometimes they survive hidden. You must find other *New Ones,* or at least Half-ones to protect him. But Half-ones are few, and fewer still are those willing to help. I would go with you, but I am too old."

"How do you know this? Are you a *New One*?"

"Come to me again, and I will tell you more."

But she did not go to White Hair, for something happened to Bough early the next morning. By the watering place—she had just stepped away from washing—a male picked up her baby and hung him upside down, dangling him over the water. The baby wailed. Bough shrieked and went into a fury. She attacked the male.

The man batted her to the ground and laughed, wiping scratches on his face. The baby thrashed in the water, and Bough fished him out. "I forget the mother is a Wild One," he said. She braced herself for another blow, but she was lucky. The male's name was Laughter. Another male would have killed her and dashed the baby to death.

The baby had lived this time, but the thing that happened was bad. Bough realized she could not stop herself from fighting a male if he threatened her child. It would happen again, for males were lingering by her tree. They would not be doing this if Sharpener had not been away for so long. White Hair was right. She must leave.

Bough went to her tree and made her plan. The next morning she would take three things: a sharp stick, a cutting stone, and a gourd for water.

She left before dawn, after the night leopard had passed. The baby was strangely quiet. Somehow, he knew, too, that a perilous journey had begun.

CHAPTER II

Hill of Offerings

Sensing her chances were small, Bough wiped tears from her face. The baby had become heavy, and she needed to rest. The stick and the baby were too heavy together, yet she kept carrying both.

Stopping in the open was risky. A predator might see them and know they were weak. She was always looking for places to hide, for when night falls, she must be in a protected place.

She was in a land of giants. A black hawk, half as large as her, landed nearby. If she had not thrust and swung her stick, the hawk would have taken her baby. Her bird friend still followed her. What could it have done?

Bough hungered, yet her breasts stayed filled for the baby. She would die before they emptied. It was the way of things. Yet she must live, if her baby was to live.

She killed her bird friend and ate it. Tears fell from her eyes. She had asked the bird for its life. The bird had trusted her and came into her hand. That was the one rule now: *My child and I must live!*

"Things have changed. A new time is coming," White Hair had said. *Yes, I need to learn to kill larger animals. I must become like a male and hunt. Yet am I not a mother?* Her life had become strange. Bough remembered the words of the old woman who had tended to her son's birth. "Ah, I have not seen one in some time, an *Early Child*!" she had pronounced, "How could you have one, you who are a child yourself!"

The old woman became sad. "I have seen many like this die." And she gave the baby back to Bough.

Later, Bough had asked her, "How do I protect him?"

"Find a male and protect the *Early Child* with sharp sticks. It may not be enough. Males come and go."

"What if there is no male? Tell me what more I can do."

The woman considered. "There is yet another thing. If you find yourself and your baby unprotected, put earth on his head and hold him up to the sky. Ask the powers to protect him. Say, 'He is yours!' He will become a *Child of the Elements*. Know that he will not just be your child, for the Elements will have a claim on him. But they will help him survive."

"No, he will be my child only!" Bough had said, clutching the baby.

She remembered the woman smiling and wondered how the Elements could claim her child. There were powers everywhere; she felt them. They could come in a sudden fury, or they could be present on a lazy day.

Night fell, and she was lucky. Among rocks, she found a narrow cleft in which they could bed. This time, she had found a place. But what of tomorrow? One day, her luck would run out, and she would not find a protected place. She knew this, but what could she do? Her only hope was to find the *New Ones* soon.

Bough retreated deeper into the opening and thought back to earlier times. She had trusted, stayed still, and the danger would pass. It was luck so far and some of her doing. Yet luck was luck; it might or might not be. Luck might miss one time, and that would be enough to die.

Morning came and Bough saw an unusual pattern of birds. She heard a distant howl. Wolves were not far away. The sky was overcast and looked angry. It did not bode well. The baby was silent, his eyes wide open.

Small One set out and came upon a piece of luck. She found an old deer carcass and rubbed herself on it. The odor of death would help hide her. She threw up, and the baby cried. Yes, her ways had changed. She would do things she would not have done before.

The sky darkened, and wind swelled up. It would rain. Bough had come to a long flat place far from any stands of trees or outcrops of rocks. There was no shelter. The death smell made her sick again. The baby began crying, sensing things were wrong.

A small herd of antelope passed in a line, and later the shadowy shapes of two lions. She quieted the baby and lay still on the ground like one dead. The lions passed, for she had the protection of the death smell.

Bough came to a stream and cleaned some. Hooves and paw prints marked the stream bank. She would have to leave soon, for dangerous animals would be coming. Following the stream, she came to where it narrowed and became rocky stretches where there were no tracks. Upending stones, she ate worms and larvae.

Bough sensed something wrong. She fled from the water. She did not see the danger. Maybe she had made it up. Still, she ran, sensing danger.

A light rain started. She was in an open field. In the distance ahead, a solitary hill was crowned with rocks. She headed toward it, cradling her baby. Somehow she moved fast, even with the baby, and she realized she had left her stick behind. Bough suddenly saw two lions to the right: the danger. But they were downwind and did not smell her. They were playing in the rain. Bough ran toward the hill. *There might be a cave among the rocks,* she thought.

When wolf howls sounded from the hill ahead of her, she stopped in her tracks. She had made a mistake and run toward wolves. Caught between lions and wolves, she and the baby would die.

What could she do? The only thing she could think to do was to stop and be still. She cried silently and tried to hold back the trembling.

The rain fell harder, and there was distant thunder. Lightning flashed. It came to her, a thing she had not done. She remembered the words of the old lady at her child's birthing.

"Offer the child. That is your best hope." Now is the time. The rain and lightning—the Elements are here!

Bough was facing death, and she had no male with her. Her baby had no name. She rubbed earth on his head and knew what she must do next.

Her tears started falling, for she sensed if she gave him to the Elements, they would one day claim him and he would die. Bough fell to her knees and sobbed. She heard the faint yapping of wolves and saw a group gathered on the far side of the hill.

She stood up in the open field, exposed. The wolves, even from the far side, might spot her. She could not remain where she was. She raced toward the hill to hide or defend herself among the rocks.

It was still raining, and there was protection in the rain, which mixed scents. Bough reached the hill and thunder rumbled. But she had some bad luck; a young pair of wolves were dangerously near. The wind would surely shift and they would scent her, even in the rain. Bough started trembling as she sensed danger engulf her.... *The baby and I will surely die.* Thunder boomed.

The time had come again; the Elements were calling. Bough knew she must act, if her baby were to live. She held him up to the sky; lightning spread and danced in the sky. Wind was sweeping the hill. "He is yours!" she cried.

It was done; the wolf pair had not yet noticed her. Bough knew she must get off the hill, but her legs remained frozen. She knew wolves saw movement better than if you were still.

The wolves were raising their noses, scenting. The rain had stopped, but the wind was shifting, stirring as if more storm was coming. She could leave behind the *Child of the Elements* and save herself, but her arms answered, clutching her child. Then, to her surprise, she heard baby crying sounds. It unbound her feet, and she moved toward the sound. She took several steps, and turned behind rocks, out of the wolves' line of sight.

Two babies were exposed on a ledge of the hill. *This is the Hill of Offerings*, she realized. *That's why the wolves are here!*

CHAPTER III

Wolf Sister

Maybe it was luck, Bough thought, for she could flee the wolves, and they would take the babies. She looked closer, and seeing a boy and girl, wondered, *Are they early children too?* It did not matter. She must leave before the wolves come. The babies had stopped crying. But how could she leave them to be eaten?

She could carry one, for she had a free hand. The boy looked sickly, pale. Bough picked up the girl child, who sounded a high-pitched wail. Bough covered her mouth and said, "Don't call the wolves!"

How did she find the strength? Bough ran down the hillside with two babies, with wind swirling at her back. She heard the wolf pack howling wildly. They had found the other baby. She turned to see the gray group milling about, their noses raised. They would soon find her scent and follow her.

Then the sky released itself; rain came in sheets and the hilltop disappeared from sight. Bough cried and laughed. The Elements were protecting them, but she had been given another to protect. It was crazy. She and her child had survived wolves, but now she had two babies to feed.

Bough sought to find a safe place as soon as she could. The lions were no longer in sight, and the wolves were silent. Perhaps they hoped that more food would come to them if they stayed on top of the hill.

Burdened, Bough made it to a stream that flooded and roared. The babies would die from the Elements, if they did not find shelter. Would the girl baby live? She was red and her wailing held life. Bough went upstream to where the water narrowed. She found an overhang that protected from the rain but was exposed to predators. She wiped and dried the babies the best she could, then fed them together.

The rain stopped, and the sun came out through a break in the sky. A faint rainbow appeared. *The Elements are pleased,* thought Bough. The horizon shone where colors met the earth, a place that seemed far away. They were still exposed, but Bough had no choice but to trust. Exhausted, she fell asleep, clutching her babies.

There was still light when Bough woke, hungry. She set out carrying the two babies in search of a safe place before the day would end. Upstream, it became rockier, and she followed a path made by animals.

The sun would soon die, and Bough scanned the rocks for shelter. They were sheer and unrelenting. Small One found a crack that opened wide enough. She fit inside, with babies to either side. By her feet, she placed some loose rocks for her defense. She was hidden from view, but a small animal might still try to enter and grab a leg or an arm. It was not a place to live, but it was the best she could do.

No beast bothered them that night. There are places that beasts do not go, and every rock is not searched. Maybe the wet had hid their scent. The small family huddled in a bundle, their warmth shared.

In the morning Bough picked up her two burdens. She washed them quickly in the stream, then went further up the rocky way. Rocks cut her feet, and once she almost fell. She walked carefully, giddy from hunger.

Bough stopped, put the babies down by the water, and knew she must find food. She overturned rocks near the stream and found a few worms. She ate them, but her stomach was so empty that she struggled not to vomit. There were plants, and she ate one that tasted safe.

The babies cried for food, so she fed them and grew weaker herself. A slow death faced her. She must find a larger and safer place to stay, lay traps for birds, and regain her strength. It was all she could think to do.

Bough saw that holes appeared in the rocks. At first they were shallow, but they deepened and looked foreboding. She needed to find a cave, one with enough deepness to retreat, and not so wide so she could defend the opening.

She found one a little way from the running water. Setting down the babies, Bough climbed up footholds in the rock and into the cave. She took a few steps in and shouted into a space which narrowed. It was empty. Then she went back and carried in one baby at a time. Last, she sat down, dizzy from hunger.

After dozing, Bough left her babies to search for food. She upturned rocks and found a few larvae. With sticks she made two bird traps, then collected brush to make a bed in the cave. She would have to name the babies herself, she thought, little names until she could find the right ones. Yet, even for this, she was too exhausted to think.

Before the day's end, Bough went out yet once more, keeping an eye on the cave opening. She looked for more food, and in the stream, she caught a crayfish. Bough was so hungry, she ate it, shell and all. Her bird traps were empty, but she found seeds and laid them in the traps. Last, she found a stick, long enough to serve as a weapon, and picked up a palm-sized stone, sharp on one side, that could crush or cut.

A day passed, and her breasts were becoming empty. *Would the babies die first?* she wondered. They would all die unless something changed. She needed to search further out to find food, but that would put the babies at risk. Somehow, she must kill a large blooded creature.

The next morning Bough found enough brush to cover the cave opening and went out to hunt. Her strength was ebbing. The babies wanted food that morning, but she had refused them. The pain pierced her, but she needed the strength to hunt.

Small One set out to find food for herself to live another day. For a terrible moment, she wondered if she should kill the girl baby to survive. She decided she could not. The baby, who had been placed on the Hill of Offering, was likely a *New One* too.

Bough searched, but found no food. Birds passed high overhead, the trees were empty, and there was no sign of ground animals. She needed some luck, but she only found a carcass filled with maggots that she could not bear to see. Bough found something that kept her from eating the maggots—a root from a water plant. She tasted it, and it was not bitter. She ate half and saved the rest.

Bough, still hungry, came back to the cave. When she spied the opening, the worst thing that she could have imagined had happened. The brush was turned aside. *An animal had entered the cave!* She should never have left the babies. They would both be dead, with only mauled bones left.

With her stick in hand, Bough climbed up and stepped into the cave. A thick animal smell, then a growl, greeted her from the dark. It sounded like a wolf, not a bear. She raised her stick and slammed it to the ground.

A high-pitched bark answered. In the dim light, she saw a young wolf lying next to her babies. There was no blood. What had happened? Was the wolf saving them for later? Bough saw something she could not explain. The girl baby was reaching out, playing with the wolf's ears.

Bough approached warily, careful not to provoke the young wolf. She talked to him, trying to make him feel safe. If she could come close enough, she could club him on the head. As she neared, the wolf stretched out his paws in greeting and whimpered. Bough was close enough to kill him now. Was that wise? What if she failed? Would he not lash out and bite at her and the babies? Maybe the wolf was not a danger.... Would he not have already eaten the babies?

The mother wolf would be the danger, Bough suddenly realized. Where was she? Then Bough understood; there was no mother. The young wolf thought this was his new den, his brother and sister. The wolf had been fooled. He was looking for a new home and had found one. And she was the mother wolf come home.

Bough slowly approached the cub and stretched out her hand to let him smell. The wolf licked her hand. The babies cried and Bough quickly gathered them in her arms and withdrew a distance. Keeping her eye on the wolf, she fed her babies with what little she had left. The wolf stared at her greedily.

After a while she fed him too. *I am to be mother to this wolf, if we are to survive*, she thought. Her baby girl was already his sister, for had she not helped tame him? Small One gave all the life she had and wondered what she could do next. She ate the rest of the tuber, then lay down exhausted. The wolf nuzzled his head next to them and slept.

The next day, Bough still had some food for her babies. The wolf was gone. There were still the bird traps. She looked out of the entrance and saw no sign of the wolf. Small One went down to the traps and found them trampled, with blood and bird feathers scattered about. The trap had worked, but the wolf had feasted.

Bough broke down and cried. She pounded her fists on the ground and raised them to the sky. "Is this how you care for your child? You let a wolf come and take our food!"

It was hopeless. The Elements could not bring her food. They could quench their thirst with water, or bring them fire, but they could not hunt for them.

Bough rebuilt the traps, then went back into the cave. The babies were hungry, and she could not give them enough. She would feed them to the end, she decided.

Somehow, they survived the rest of the day, but Bough had no strength to leave the cave on the next. The babies cried, but there was no more. Death was coming. "Sleep babies," she said as she drifted off.

It was still light when Bough woke to a wolf's muffled yap. She clutched her stick. The beast would have no more. This was their last hope, for her to kill the wolf. Bough struggled to her knees and raised the stick.

CHAPTER IV
Rabbit Mouth

The wolf had a rabbit in its mouth, Bough suddenly saw. His mouth was bloody, but he had not eaten it. Why did the wolf do this?

Bough gently summoned the wolf, and he grudgingly let the rabbit go by her feet. Thanking the wolf, she took the rabbit and used her stone to cut it up. Bough ate the rabbit raw and felt life coursing through her. "You ate my birds, so I will eat your rabbit." Still, she gave a leg back to the wolf. "Good work, Rabbit Mouth. You are part of my family."

The wolf licked the blood from the cave floor and looked at her, his eyes having a sudden intensity. *What will we do when he grows large?* she wondered.

Bough and her babies would survive for a time more. It seemed like luck and something more than luck. Rabbit Mouth helped to protect them, and just when they would start feeling hunger, he would bring them food. He even learned not to take from the traps. Still, Bough fed him a bird every so often.

As time went on, Rabbit Mouth would spend a full day away and not bring back food. Perhaps there was not much food to be had, for the wolf's ribs showed. Small One and her two children were starving again, but something unexpected saved them. One morning they woke to undulating, whirring sounds. Hundreds of insects were crawling out of the earth, and many were flying and falling from the sky. Although winged, they were slow on the ground or hardly seemed to move. She saved them in the dark, cool portions of the cave. They were food and there was plenty. Rabbit Mouth ate them as well.

So, Bough and the wolf kept their strength, and her babies grew. The boy crawled about in the cave. They changed so fast. He quickly learned new sounds and was making his own. The girl, a little younger, followed in his ways.

Rabbit Mouth grew bigger, and Bough feared the day when he would forget his young ways. What would she do then? They needed the wolf, for predators avoided his scent, and he would still sometimes bring them food. He began spending two and three days away. When he would come back, it seemed that each time, he had grown and that his eyes were changing.

One day when Rabbit Mouth was away, Bough climbed down from the cave to check on her traps by the stream. When she turned to go back, she saw near the cave's mouth a tan cat as large as her. The night cat was hungry, for it was out in the day. And Bough saw it was a mother with enlarged teats, so she would be doubly hungry. The cat must have ranged far to find food for her young. But the mother cat had smelled wolf about and did not enter the cave right away.

Small One grabbed a stick that lay on the ground and beat it against rocks. The night cat turned to consider the threat, hissing and tensing. Bough threw stones and when one skidded up to the cat's feet, she jumped away. The feline went around her and crossed the stream, awaiting amid the brush. Bough rushed up to the cave.

The night cat had been held off for now. Yet, if Rabbit Mouth stayed away this night, the cat would try to take them in the dark. The mother cat was hungry and had found food. She would be patient and wait.

Bough realized that even if the cat gave up now and left, she would remember where to return. The cat could come any night, and how would she be prepared? The night cat was still; maybe it was asleep.

Small One knew the animal was only doing what she was, trying to feed her young. The desperate thought came to her: *I could leave the girl child and flee with my boy.* But she couldn't do that, for the girl had become her child too. They were all like one now. And would not the cat, fed once, expect more and follow them?

The day was waning, and the time passed when Rabbit Mouth would have come back. In the twilight, the odds were shifting the cat's way.

Bough would stay awake for the night, but then the day would come and she would need to sleep. Small One decided she would take a big risk and face the cat. She could think of no plan, except a bad one. If she limped, acted as if wounded, then be still as death, she could fool the cat into drawing close, and kill it with her stick. But if she did not hit a forceful first blow, she would find a cat with strong jaws and claws at her throat.

There was no time to think further. Bough went out of the cave in the waning light, the day ending sooner than she thought. She stood still, but could not bring herself to feign death. She stared at the night cat, and the cat stared back.

Bough shook for fear. In a few bounds, she would be dead and her babies defenseless. Her legs trembled, although she knew she mustn't shake. Bough bit her tongue, drawing blood, and her shaking stopped. She feared she could not stop it much longer.

The night cat was a predator and did not expect her prey to stare back. But the cat held her ground and waited.

Knowing that time was short before her trembling returned, Bough screamed and waved her stick wildly. "Go away, mother cat! Find some others to feed your young! You will not have mine!" She threw a stone as far as she could and it landed, skittering up to the cat.

The night cat had seen enough. No animal prey had done such things. Backing away from this strangeness, the cat melted into the night. She could come back another day.

Bough fell to her knees, her trembling released. How long she stayed there, she did not know.

The next thing she remembered was that she was in the cave, with Rabbit Mouth lying next to her. It was morning, and she scolded him. "Why were you away when we needed you? Why do you leave your family for so long?"

Then she noticed Rabbit Mouth had blood on his muzzle and his side bore claw marks. So, Rabbit Mouth had a fight with the night cat after all. That was good. The cat would think twice before coming back. Bough laughed. "Your name has changed, Cat Mouth."

BOUGH'S FAMILY HAD gained time and would not have to rush away. The boy was walking, and the girl crawled. Bough could envision a time when they would be ready to leave. Still, she worried. She knew it would be best to leave while the wolf was still young and would listen. How else would they make it across an open, dangerous stretch? How would they ever reach others like themselves? To stay here too long would not do. And if one cat found them, would not another? Yet her children needed to gain more size and strength before they could journey.

A full moon came and went without event. The boy was strong enough to walk for stretches now. He spoke words like hers and found new ones as well. Bough listened and wondered. Some words she half knew, and some she didn't. When he said his first word again, Manwey, she decided it was one of his names.

The girl imitated the boy, but she added her own sounds, ones she spoke to the wolf. Bough smiled and did not frown, for she knew her children were different. She took care to teach the girl about animals, to tell her stories with the wolf, who yapped and made moaning sounds. The girl was quick and learned wolf-talk. Although Cat Mouth sometimes played with the boy, the girl child was like his sister. And if she were to name her, she decided, it would be Wolf Sister.

As for Manwey, he was still a *Child of the Elements*, and Bough would take him out into the wind and rain, even when it thundered and showed lightning. The boy loved the rain and wind. He would make noises like rain, wind, and thunder—swishing and trilling sounds and the deepest sounds he could manage. When it rained, he would raise his hands high over his head like he was joining the sky.

Cat Mouth was changing too. Although Bough took great care to be kind to the wolf, he would stay away for even longer. Often too, when the wolf came back, his mouth was bloody and empty of food. Bough would scold the wolf then, and sometimes he would growl back. She showed no fear, although her legs weakened. Cat Mouth was now half her size and could easily kill her.

Sometimes when the wolf played, he would knock her over and mouth her neck. The trembling almost started then. There were other signs. At night, instead of sleeping with them, the wolf slept at the entrance. The time was coming when the wolf would leave and not come back.

Bough thought hard about what she would do then. A stick—she had made a new one—helped to keep her authority. She had used a stick on him once, when he was younger. She dared not strike him now. One thing helped more than any other, to keep the wolf tame. Cat Mouth still played and nuzzled with the girl child. It seemed the wolf knew she was his sister.

The time came when her family must set out. Manwey was strong enough to walk a good distance before he needed to rest. Would Cat Mouth follow? They would be on the move at least, and she felt it was what the wolf wanted. It was a chance she would have to take.

The day came. The wolf had come home with a rabbit, like he had the first time. That was a good sign. Bough praised the wolf and gave half the rabbit back.

After eating, she picked up Wolf Sister, not too heavy to carry. Manwey was eager to go. Cat Mouth followed, thinking they were going to search for food like they sometimes did. When they went further than they had ever gone, Cat Mouth ran back and forth, happy. He was roaming like his wolf nature wanted him to do.

Did Cat Mouth know he had no real pack to defend him? There would be jackals, hyenas, lions and great birds. Still, together they would have a chance.

CHAPTER V

Howler

It was slow going, for Wolf Sister was heavy. There was no time to trap birds, and Bough relied on chance finds: eggs, tubers, insects, and whatever small prey Cat Mouth could snatch.

It was amazing, for Cat Mouth still saw her as pack leader.

The land became scrappy, the trees fewer and further between. That was good and bad, for it meant fewer predators and less food. She saw horned animals on the horizon, small burrowing animals that disappeared as they approached, and circling hawks.

At night they would sleep in trees, although it was hard to carry the children. Once in the tree, Bough would hold the girl close, but Manwey had learned to balance himself.

Bough heard him say something surprising while they were up in the tree. "We wolf." Then he howled, and the wolf howled too. Wolf Sister didn't need encouragement to join. It was the strangest thing.

Yet, it helped save them. Once, while walking at midday, six jackals approached. Bough knew they could not defend themselves against so many. So, she told the boy and girl to howl, and the wolf joined them. It sounded like many wolves, and the jackals turned away.

My boy has gained a new name, Howler, thought Bough. *He too is a brother of wolves.*

Bough led her family eastward, the way White Hair had said to go, although the land became drier and sparser. They became hungry, and Bough wondered how they would survive, and what Cat Mouth would do. Would the wolf just wander off? Sometimes, after they had awakened, he wanted to go a different way.

When Bough set out, she would turn and call, "Cat Mouth! Come with Howler and your Wolf Sister."

The wolf would look at them for several moments, then trot on and join them.

The family became thirsty, and Bough found only occasional plants to chew. She still fed both children, but she knew the land must change soon, or they would die. If they became too weak to travel, the vultures would come.

Bough let the wolf decide for a time and they veered off the eastern path. Soon, they came upon a half-dried pond where sprouts grew by slips of water. On one side, large rocks loomed, places to sleep. Tracks of dangerous animals were present, but Bough was happy to have found water and shelter.

In the pond the children got wet and muddy, and Howler played with Cat Mouth. It got rough, and the wolf knocked Howler over. He rose, screaming, and hit the wolf.

Cat Mouth snap-barked and almost drew blood from Howler's arm.

Bough shouted and came toward the wolf with her stick raised. Cat Mouth was the stronger, but he backed away. Later, fearless Wolf Sister hugged the wolf, and he calmed.

Still, Bough was left shaken. Although the wolf showed no further anger, she sensed that things had changed.

Bough knew Cat Mouth was becoming too dangerous. He had lost his puppy ways and wanted to hunt and range the way wolves do. Maybe, too, he realized they were not wolves. Recently, they had found no food but plants, and wolves do not eat plants.

That night, Bough and her children slept under a boulder that formed an arching hollow. Cat Mouth slept a distance away. Bough dreamed that she and her children were attacked by a bear. She called for Cat Mouth, who went to their defense. The wolf died, and the wounded bear crawled away. In the dream they ate their wolf brother.

Bough woke wondering, *Is the dream telling me we must eat Wolf to survive?* She decided she could not. He had saved their lives more than once. And though Cat Mouth was a wolf, he was also part of their family. Besides, what would happen if she only wounded him? She decided she must send the wolf away.

That morning the wolf wanted to leave a different way and Bough let him. For a moment Cat Mouth had hesitated, turning to look their way, but she did not call for him. Cat Mouth disappeared, and their hope for survival seemed to disappear with him.

When Sister Wolf fully realized the risk, she cried out for the wolf, but it was too late.

Was it the right or wrong thing to do? she wondered. So far they had both luck and the wolf. Was it a bad time for the wolf to leave? Open land lay ahead and would not a dangerous animal come soon?

Bough decided they should stay for a time by water, so she looked for a safer home among the rocks. She found a raised hollow that could be defended at night. Then, as she was setting bird traps by the pond, she saw the fading print of an adult human. Her heart quickened, and hope raced through her. *Perhaps New Ones will come to us! Sometimes not moving was like moving.*

The next day, birds came that were too large for the traps. Lizards scampered by, who were too quick to capture. In the evening, a lone leopard watered and sniffed about. The scent was confused, and the leopard left to follow the lone wolf's direction.

"Good luck, Brother Wolf. You're on your own. I hope you find a new pack soon."

CHAPTER VI

A New Skin

The hollow proved a suitable place to stay, and Bough bided her time. Sister Wolf must become old enough to walk on her own. A moon came and went, and Bough learned to kill small burrowing animals.

Manwey was speaking more and putting words together in new ways. After Bough said, "The sun is coming up," he would say, "The sun is opening its eye." When she said, "The water is rushing by today," he would say the water is speaking, "Come with me today." She did not correct him, for her son was a New One.

As for the girl, she was from others and different from the boy. But Bough had saved her, so the girl was at least half hers. Bough wondered how one who had been almost eaten by wolves had become a friend of wolves.

"There are questions which cannot be answered," White Hair had once told her. Then she remembered the boy was only half hers too, for he was given to the Elements. The fear came to her. *Wouldn't the Elements claim him one day? Won't the wolves try to claim the girl too? Things, she knew, have a way of coming back.*

Bough tried to look ahead, but the future was dim. One thing came to her, however. *Howler and Wolf Sister should always stay together and help each other in life. They are both New Ones. But that is far away in time, and one cannot see that far.*

Bough stayed one moon longer. It rained, and the pond did not dry up. Frogs appeared, and for once there was plenty to eat. Wolf Sister liked to call upon the small animals and birds. Sometimes rabbits would come near to her without fear. Bough would not kill these. "One cannot kill friends," she would say.

They had close calls. One time a striped hyena attacked her before she could raise herself up in the hollow. His jaws kept leaping at her, and Bough fiercely fended him off with her stick. Her arms were left slashed and bitten.

Bough did her best to teach her children how to survive. One day, Howler was in the stream, and his foot got caught between rocks. Bough freed him, using a stick to pry the rocks open. The boy could have used his own stick. Bough taught him: "When you cannot do something, look for another way. Remember, you are a *New One*!"

Once, Wolf Sister found a hurt bird near the pond and brought it to Bough. The bird's leg was bent and could not walk. Bough thought to wrap the leg with a stick and some vine. Wolf Sister cared for the bird and fed it. After a couple days, the bird could stand. Bough took off the splint, and the bird flew away. *A sign,* thought Bough, and she said to Wolf Sister. "You helped make the bird well. You have a gift."

One day, Wolf Sister went missing, and Bough searched everywhere. She found her on a little knoll, next to two baby animals with horns.

I have different children, thought Bough. *But this trait of Wolf Sister could mean trouble. If she does not fear animals, what will happen if a great cat comes?* Bough tried to teach her to be wary of predators, but Wolf Sister did not seem to understand. She could walk now, and the boy could run. Was it not time to move on?

To test luck in the open without their wolf friend would be dangerous. Yet to stay by the pond was dangerous, too. In time, a predator would catch them off guard. There was no good choice.

Everything changed one day when they heard voices by the pond. Two men, a woman, and a half-grown male were putting their skin packs by the pond. Bough remained hidden among the rocks, for the Sharpener had warned about the *Eaters of Others*. These four were different from her people, for they had deer skins hanging on them. *Why do they wear the skins of the ones they eat?*

Bough watched as the group searched the ground and cast their eyes about, looking and wondering who had left fresh tracks. One man followed the markings toward them, but lost the path among the rocks and returned.

Should she appear to them? They did not look like hunters of her kind. Maybe these were the *New Ones* for whom they were looking. How could she be sure? No one had told her what they looked like, only that they would be different. She had to take a chance, she decided.

Bough waited until the group was readying to leave. Summoning her courage, she left her children behind and went to greet them. If they were hostile, she would lead them away from her children.

Bough, carrying her stick, stopped when they saw her.

For a long moment, they looked at her. She heard them speak words, some of which she could not make out.

"Look! A Wild One...?"

"If she ... be careful."

"No, her stick is not raised."

"She still carries one, and ... She looks like a Wild One."

"Lower your sticks," said the woman in the group. "If she is simple, she will think we mean to harm her. After all, we are four."

"Stay ready," ordered their leader, who wore a leopard skin. "I do not want to be poked by such a one. The smallest can be the fiercest."

Bough made out most of this, and it made her angry. She would only attack if they tried to hurt her or her children. She clenched her stick and kept her look determined.

The group stood still and stared, uncertain.

"She has no skins; she is not our kind," said the other grown man. "It is best to leave untamed ones alone. She must be wild, to be by herself."

"How can she be that fierce?" asked the woman. "She is small, hardly grown herself. And her stick is not raised."

The leader's voice was traced with anger. "Could you sleep at night with such a one next to you? Look at her eyes. She has killed animals, maybe her own kind. We had best leave."

"No, wait--look!" cried the woman.

Out of the rocks a boy came running. Howler joined his mother's side with his stick raised to defend her.

Bough used her hand to lower her son's stick. They were at the mercy of this group. She could see that they did not want to kill her, nor did they want to take her with them. Something was wrong. Was she too different? She remained at a distance, not knowing what to do.

Then Bough started trembling. She had fought against it, for if she trembled she could not fight or run. She had done so much to survive, and this was her children's best chance. Yet the group did not want them. She fought back tears as they moved to leave. They were not ones who would harm her or her children.

"Don't go!" she yelled. "Take my child." She pushed the boy forward.

"A Wild One who can speak," said the surprised leader.

"And a mother willing to give us her child," added the woman. "We must take the child at least. It is our way to protect the Little Ones. She is alone with a child, and he would die in time. Yet if we take him, how can we leave her?"

The boy in their group spoke, "There must be others of her kind. How else can she have survived?"

"That is true," said the leader. "Yet there are no others, for she would not have shown herself to us. As it is, she has only this little one. But we know she is not our kind."

The woman came to Small One's defense. "She may not be our kind, but she must be a good defender. The boy looks healthy. She knows how to survive and protect. She is both mother and hunter. See the scars on her arms and her body. Have you seen as many on a male hunter?"

Those were strong words in Bough's favor. Still, decisions like this were not made quickly or easily. The group stood still, the leader deciding, and his head shook no. Then the girl child came out, toddling to the mother.

"Two children!" cried the troop, amazed.

The girl child clung to her mother and cast a scared, fierce look.

The leader exclaimed, "This is too much! How could this group have survived? And where could they be going?"

To their surprise, the boy answered, "We go to the sun's waking eye."

"What, a *New One*?" immediately exclaimed the woman. "He is like us! We must take him!"

"And the Trembling One?"

The woman's anger rose. "I know she is wild. But she has courage, has she not? Who knows what animals she has had to fight off? And if she has birthed a New One, then she must be a Halfling herself."

"It could be as Gazelle says," said the leader, revealing the woman's name. "We have helped Half-ones in the past."

The other man raised a concern. "Are not Half-ones a risk, for they don't know our ways and reveal too much to others. Look how much she has said to us. But I do not doubt that the two young ones can be taught in our ways."

The leader paused only a moment more before deciding. "We will take all three. It is our way. Give this mother hunter a greeting and a new skin."

The men stayed behind while the woman drew up to Bough. She made a sign of greeting, and Bough remained still, not knowing how to respond. The woman named Gazelle smiled, reached out, and touched her arm.

Bough clutched her stick, but she let the woman hold her arm.

"You will take them?" asked Bough.

"Yes, and you too!" Gazelle replied. "We are now your family. We are not like the ones who range about and kill. You need not fear us."

The woman held out a gazelle skin and wrapped it around Bough. At first she was confused, thinking she was being restrained, but the skin just hung around her.

"It is our way," Gazelle said, when she saw Bough's confused look. "Come, we have much to show you. What is your boy's name?"

That, Bough understood. "He is Howler."

"Oh, we must give him a more peaceful name. And what is the girl's?"

Bough blushed. "I found her among wolves, so I call her Wolf Sister. She is a child."

Gazelle laughed. "Of course, she is a child, and a beautiful child at that. Wolf Sister is not a bad name, and it can be one. We will also give her a new one."

"What is yours?" the woman finally asked. "You have heard mine."

Bough hesitated. These *New Ones* were trying to change everything. They had wrapped a skin around her and were planning to give her children new names. She fingered the skin, wanting to tear it off. She would flee and take her children with her. Small One stared at the strange faces around her and her panic grew. Her trembling started again. No, she wouldn't let them take her children! She raised her staff off the ground.

The men instantly steeled, gripping their sticks.

Gazelle, however, stroked her. "It is all right, Wild One. We will not take your children away. Come with us, and they will be yours. We will help protect you and your children. Please tell us your name."

CHAPTER VII

Left Behind

It had been a long time since Bough had been touched by an adult. She looked into the woman's eyes and didn't see any intention to hurt. She saw something she couldn't quite name. Gazelle was gazing at her with the love of a parent. Her trembling ceased. If this woman were this kind to her, the men might not treat her badly. She remembered what it was like to be a child. "My name is Bough," she finally said.

What else could she do? Times had changed, and one must do what was necessary. She need not reveal her other names—Small One, Trembling One, or Woman to the Sharpener. Leaving the skin-wrap on, she walked with the woman.

Bough accepted the names of the men—how could she refuse? Their leader was Long Ears, and like the Long-Eared Owl, he listened and fought well. Daring Hawk was brave and took risks. The older boy's name was Water Otter, for he was long and lithe, and liked to swim.

"Come, it is time to go," announced Long Ears, and he pointed toward the sun.

The group traveled with the sun, some to the right, and Bough asked, "Are there more *New Ones* this way?"

"We are all that are left of our group, for many have died," Gazelle revealed. "We hope to find more groups of New Ones this way."

Could this be all the New Ones left? Would they not need more to survive? Bough's group had many times this.

"Did you have any young ones?" asked Bough.

The woman became sad. "It is hard for young to live when you are traveling. Our babies are born weak and the night animals take them. How you and your young have survived is a mystery to us. Maybe you have protection from the powers."

"What powers do you speak of?" asked Bough.

"I forget a Half-one may not know. There are many powers we sense. You must have some feeling for them. When the wind blows, when it storms, do you not feel them?"

Bough wanted to tell about her boy, but she would not give up his name so easily. "I know there are powers and there is luck," she answered.

"Yes, there is luck...." Gazelle sighed. "Lately, we have had little. Maybe you can help change that. The powers have not been with us lately. We will need both the powers and luck to make it."

"Long Ears thinks we can make it across the drylands with your two young ones. He knows the safest way. It will not be easy. Keep your stick ready."

Amid the scrubland, smaller rocks were strewn about. The New Ones were always scanning the horizon and checking for tracks. The younger male was friendly and got along well with the boy. Water Otter eyed Bough at times, but she looked the other way. She belonged to the Sharpener, even if he was not near.

Bough walked with Gazelle and felt less alone. The vigilance she always had was no longer necessary. The woman held her hand and sometimes carried her child. Bough melted from the woman's kindness.

Daring Hawk kidded Gazelle, "You have found another child? A halfling mother, a fierce hunter! Will you be able to tamer her?"

Gazelle smiled back and warned, "Be careful, or my Small One will bite you."

Bough wondered how the woman knew one of her names and how she had been defended. These people allowed a woman to defend with words. *That is a good thing. One can do something other than remain silent or fight.*

When the men saw fresh leopard tracks, their course altered, and they veered directly toward the eastern sun. This change in path was not taken easily, and the group spent much time deciding.

The land became more barren, with little food about. There was no sign of any more leopard tracks, but they still hurried. The *New Ones* rested by a small waterhole surrounded by a harsh emptiness. They kept watch, with clear sight around. Sometimes, the New Ones cast an anxious gaze her way.

"I see or smell nothing. What is it?" asked Bough.

Gazelle looked to Long Ears, who nodded, and she went on to explain. "An old, hungry lion lives in these parts. Long-Tooth has killed one of our young before. He does this because he cannot catch other animals. If he sees us in the open, he will try to do it again."

An alarm went off within Bough. *What about my young?*

"We call him Ragged Ears because he has survived many fights," Gazelle went on. "Still, we are clever and have found ways to evade him."

Bough suddenly became wary of the *New Ones. Why did the troop go this way? Were they planning to use one of my young ones to gain passage?*

The woman spoke as if she knew Bough's worries. "The other way has many fierce leopards. One or more of us would surely die then. The old lion has this territory, and we have passed unharmed before."

Her children may have still figured into their plans, Bough couldn't help thinking. What else could she expect? The group would do what was necessary to survive. New young ones could come into the world again, but all would die if the adults died.

"If you need, you can leave me for the lion," Bough abruptly offered. "He will not have my children!"

Gazelle laughed, but seeing that Bough was serious, considered.

Had they offered one of their own before? Bough wondered, and she tremored with tears in her eyes. She did not want to die.

Gazelle woman stroked Bough, and her tremors ceased. "Do not fear. The old lion sleeps a lot. But we need to reach shelter before the night falls.

"One time before, I offered myself, but I am a *New One* who can bear a child. The men will protect me with their lives. You are half *New One,* but their instinct will be to protect you too. We will find a way."

"How can we kill a large lion?" asked Bough. "I have only fought wildcats before."

"Yes, I see." Gazelle's eyes held amazement as she considered the size of animals that Bough must have fought.

"There is not much use fighting a lion in the open," admitted Gazelle, and her face became crossed with pain.

She must have lost a young to the lion already, Bough realized, and she hugged the woman for the first time.

The surprised woman returned the hug, and they held each other. The men glanced their way, but said nothing.

Long Ears got up, and their journey continued. There were no fresh tracks about, only days-old wolf tracks.

It was late in the day when Long Ears pointed to the horizon. In the haze, a form was moving on the horizon. The lion had come.

It was the worst possible place, for they were still in open land, with not a rock in sight.

Bough said to the others, "I will die to save my young."

The old lion was ranging close, but not too close.

Long Ears spoke: "Ragged Ears will wait for the night, when he will see better than us. We have a little time yet to find shelter."

Bough objected. "There's no place in sight. Leave me. I will make camp here, and the lion will stalk me. At night I will face him. Take my children and go."

"You will not live," said Gazelle.

"The lion will have me, but all the New Ones will escape. I know there is no luck with a lion."

"Come with us. We have powers to call upon."

"My boy has powers, too. Take him with you!"

The *New Ones* considered all this.

Then Long Ears said, "It is not for a woman to fight a lion. Still, it is a plan for the young and the New Ones to survive."

"She is the mother!" cried Gazelle. Yet in her protest, she knew this plan might work.

"How can we stop her, if she is willing?" asked their leader. "It is the right of the mother to protect her children any way she can."

Daring Hawk stepped forward. "But it is not our way to leave a woman, even a Half-one, to fight a lion alone. I will stay with her. Maybe together, we can kill the lion."

Bough felt amazement at this, that a male would risk his life for her.

"No," said Long Ears. "You would be killed too. We need a plan for which the most might live."

Daring Hawk's face was set. It did not seem right that Bough should show as much courage as he. Yet, he knew that Long Ear's words held truth. There was little hope with two against a lion, even if he were old.

Long Ears spoke again with a tone that brokered no disagreement. "Stay with the group. We will need you for the battles ahead to keep the New Ones alive."

Daring Hawk stepped back. He looked at Bough anew, as if seeing her for the first time. She was not only a hunter, but a warrior too.

The New Ones made preparations, scattering their scent and tracks about, and made beds with rocks that looked like sleeping forms.

The New Ones talked about the Half-one with respect. She may be a woman and a Halfling, but she was willing to face a lion alone. The men came to her and made special gestures for the coming battle. They cut their arms and marked her face with their blood.

"You are a warrior," Long Ears pronounced, and they gave her a sharpened stick like those they carried.

At first, Otter protested, "Can a woman be called warrior?"

"Fighting and facing death knows neither man nor woman," said Long Ears. "It is our time to leave."

Gazelle came to give Bough a parting hug.

"Do not touch her," said Long Ears. "She is dedicated."

Gazelle cried, not wanting to leave her behind, but the men pressed on.

When Gazelle picked up Wolf Sister, Bough raised no protest. Daring Hawk picked up Howler, who put up a fierce fight.

He kicked and screamed, "No! I will fight the lion too!"

Bough was proud of Howler, and she directed him. "Go with the *New Ones*. You must help them fight the animals that lay ahead."

"How will you kill the great cat alone?" asked the boy.

Bough did not know how to answer. She could not say, "A lion who has eaten will no longer be hungry." Yet she must say some last words he would remember.

"I have luck on my side," she finally answered, not believing it would work. "I will see you again."

The boy stopped resisting, and the troop walked away with him.

"Remember your names!" Bough cried out to them.

Small One turned and gazed at the yellow shape of the lion. She had known peace for a short while with the *New Ones*. Now she was left behind to die.

CHAPTER VIII

The Lion's Decision

Tears welled in Bough's eyes, but she remained alert. The old saber-tooth was waiting. She made noises to let him think that more than one human was there.

Bough felt alone, knowing she would soon die. She looked behind her, and saw the New Ones, like dots in the distance. "Protect my child!" she called after them.

When Bough turned back around, the lion was close enough to see the color of his eyes.

Ragged Ears, however, did not attack right away. He was careful, watching to see if there was any sign of a trap or danger. A wound or a simple break in his bones would likely doom him.

Bough tried to think of tricks, but there were none that could save her life. She looked to the sky, empty of Elements to defend her. She yelled, struck the ground with her stick and stirred up dust to let the lion know she had fight, that she had crazy fight in her. She must gain as much time as possible. That would be her victory.

An idea came to her when she recognized a plant whose single leaf could kill you. Maybe she could eat some leaves, and the lion would die when he ate her.

She decided against this. She would not be able to eat enough to kill a large lion. Maybe too, he would not eat her if she was already dead, for some animals were like that. It was better to fight, to give the lion a fresh kill and satisfy his hunger. Maybe she could also wound the lion, so he could not follow the others. But how could she wound a great lion?

Night was falling, and Bough sensed the lion's impatience. His torn ears shifted, and he rose. Bough howled like a wolf, as loud as she could.

Ragged Ear's vision was not so good. He did not scent wolves, yet maybe there was one. The lion lay back down to wait and see if a wolf would appear.

I have won a little more time, thought Bough. *I must think of something new.*

Nothing came to mind, however. Bough readied herself, stood up, and her body started trembling. She tried to stop it. Fire lit her mind, and she fell down, blacking out.

When Bough woke, it was dark and the old lion was breathing over her. She remained deathly still. A moment more, and he laid down beside her. *This is the strangest way to fight,* thought Bough, *but I am gaining time.*

The rising moon cast silver light upon them, and Bough dared not move. She glimpsed at her stick, just out of reach. Why had the lion not eaten her? Maybe he had learned not to eat the dead, for he had gotten sick afterwards. He was a wise lion.

But she would eventually move. Ragged Ears was patient. Sometimes he would turn his head and snort over her.

Bough was afraid, too afraid to tremble, and she wetted the gazelle skin. *Yes, I am still winning more time for the others.* Bough's imagination ran wild as she went in and out of a daze.

Dawn came and vultures circled.

Ragged ears roared. The vultures went higher, and Bough's body felt prickly. The lion got up, nudged her, and licked her. Then his paw raked her body, like thorns of fire. Bough held back her scream, but a moan escaped her. Her blood came out freshly. It was not from deep wounds, nor were they shallow. Still, the lion did not eat her. He was looking up.

Two wolves were howling. *The animals of the desert smell blood. They will feast on what the lion leaves behind. The lion will surely hurry and kill me now before other wolves come.*

The lion's ears were up, and he scented. He did not fear a couple of wolves, and it was not likely they would challenge him.

All the while, Bough dared not to move. She thought of fighting, but fight had left her.

The two wolves drew closer, and she heard their barks and snarls. *Would they fight the lion for her? Or were they testing the old lion to see if he would flee? If he did not, they would have to wait for what was left of her. They must be hungry to draw so close. Maybe they would even challenge Ragged Ears and kill him.*

She glimpsed her eyes open and saw that the wolves were waiting. *Her bones would have flesh left; they would be cracked for marrow.*

Impatient, Ragged Ears roughly nosed her. Bough could no longer control herself and started trembling. The lion pawed once more at her side, then dragged her by the arm.

A sharp growl caused the lion to stop. In an instant Ragged Ears had dropped her and turned to face the wolf. Bough could not believe that the male wolf was challenging the lion.

Bleeding, she sat up, her arms around her knees. The male had come dangerously close to the lion, risking himself for his hunger.

If they fought with each other, she might escape. But she would be weak from her wounds. It would be foolish to run for a few bounds before the lion or wolves sealed her fate.

Bough picked up her stick. At least she could get in a blow before she died. The great lion ignored her, snarling and wondering why a wolf was troubling him.

The male wolf did not back down. Then a fight of sorts began, with snarling, snapping, and brief contact––the way of many fights in the wild. The male wolf must have sensed the lion was old and that he had a chance. The female wolf remained at a distance, and Bough saw she was pregnant. She must be very hungry and the reason the male wolf risked himself.

The old lion did not like this. He had come for easy food, and wolves threatened him. Already the lion had a slight limp from old wounds. His head turned to the side, and he considered giving up his prey. The wolf acted vicious. The lion would win, but the wolf might injure him.

When Ragged Ears looked Bough's way, she struck the ground with her stick and shouted. Then she threw the stick, just missing. The old lion had seen enough and walked away.

"Fight!" cried Bough, amazed at the lion's cowardness.

There was nothing she could do. The wolf turned toward her. She would die by a wolf now. She had no stick, and there was no fight left in her. She fell to her knees and put her face in her hands.

CHAPTER IX

Lion Mouth

Bough closed her eyes and waited for death. She had done all she could do. She had faced a lion, and he had backed off. *I have won the New Ones time,* she thought. *My children have new parents now.... Protect my children,* she asked, as if the *New Ones* could hear her.

Bough waited, but the wolf was biding his time. She smelled him, knew he was near. She heard him panting, for he was right next to her. Still, she did not feel the wolf's teeth. There was nothing left to defend her. Why did the wolf wait? Her blood must be screaming to him. She opened her eyes.

The wolf had sat down beside her.

Then she recognized a mark. It was Cat Mouth, fully grown.

Bough smiled and reached out her hand, "Cat Mouth, you found me!"

She wondered if he would growl or snap, but the wolf let her stroke him as she had done before. She spoke to him, but he did not return with any sounds. Then the wolf stood up, sounded a great howl, and went to his partner.

Bough could not believe her good luck. It was Wolf Sister's doing. She had tamed Cat Mouth, and he had remembered her even though much time had passed.

Bough realized Cat Mouth saw her as part of his pack and so had defended her. The wolf's name changed again. *He is Lion Mouth now.*

Bough knew her danger was acute. She must catch up to her group, who had gone some distance in the remaining light. She was bloodied and her scent would attract beasts. *I cannot die after this! If only Lion Mouth had come with me....*

Bough left her stick behind and half-walked, half-ran. The less time in the open, the less chance to be killed. The sky was overcast, and a light rain fell. Her wounds left her streaked, but she had stopped bleeding, with long clotted stripes across her body.

In the morning twilight, Bough came to them near naked and bloodied, collapsing in their midst.

The New Ones could not believe what they saw. Had could a Halfling woman fight a lion and survive? They tended her wounds, gave her a new skin, and allowed her children to come near to her. The New Ones were amazed that none of the children cried. Maybe it was because they had seen their mother with wounds before and had seen her rise to live.

The *New Ones* feared. "Although she's a Halfling, she must have special powers to survive a lion," said Gazelle. "Maybe she is one of the *Powers* herself!"

Long Ears doubted. "Does a *Power* bleed? And why would a *Power* come to a small woman? Yes, something has happened; we do not know what. Maybe it was luck, for she always spoke of that."

Facing the lion and running wounded in the rain had been too much for Bough. She became sick and feverish, and only parts of her story came out. They heard about a wolf who had come and stood with her against the lion. There was something, too, about Lion's Mouth.

Daring Hawk interpreted: "The wolf must have died and fed the lion. That is how she survived."

"She has a wolf smell," said Long Ears, "but wounds from a lion."

"Does it matter how she survived?" asked Gazelle. "We must keep her alive!"

"It matters whether the lion is dead or wounded," their leader replied. "Will he come, following her blood? We need to leave. We cannot tend to her. The group must survive."

Gazelle protested strongly, "I will not leave her! We take her, or I will stay. If I must, I will carry her! Is she not a mother, a hunter, and a warrior? Are these three things not enough?"

"Warriors give their life for the group," said Long Ears.

"So, you would let her give herself twice?" Gazelle was enraged, fierce, and none of the men answered her more.

Bough knew that her life was being decided. Sick and alone, she would die within the day. Gazelle was her only defender and was acting as if she were her child. Yet she was not. Her own children had their heads close to hers and seemed to know what was being decided.

The men were stronger, but who was or was not with the group was a woman thing. Gazelle made earth markings on her forehead. "She is one of us," she declared. "She has the protection of women. You cannot leave her now!"

"We will carry her," Long Ears relented. "For she is marked three times: blood by our hunters, wound marks by a lion, and earth by our woman."

"It will slow us down," said Daring Hawk. "But maybe even a wounded Halfling has powers."

"If not powers," Otter offered. "She must have luck."

"By whatever means, we have passed the lion," Long Ears concluded. It was the best face he could put on a decision he would not have made.

The *New Ones* carried Bough. It slowed them down, but no lion appeared to follow them. Sometimes they heard distant howls, and Bough thought Lion Mouth was protecting her from a distance.

Bough felt weak, her wounds on fire. Gazelle fed her what she could, but there was no meat and only a little water.

She overheard talk. "Why feed one who will die?"

Will I die? Bough wondered. She had survived the lion, but she was weak from something more than the lion's claws. How could she slay this invisible thing? It did not matter, for her children would survive.

Bough was carried in the men's arms, shifted between them. Long Ears held her more gently, and Daring Hawk was stronger. Bough had not been held by men in a long while.

Sometimes she shook. Small One realized her trembling was different this time. It was from sickness that she felt hot and dry. Things around her shifted in waves of color. She was dying, she knew.

Her children, walking at her side, were silent, sensing things.

"Leave me behind," she told Gazelle. They were resting, and her mind had become clear. "I am a burden."

Gazelle stroked her. "You are one of us, and we have our ways. Even if you are to die, we must leave you at a special place."

"What is this place?"

"It is where powers come and go. I know, for I have the gift of seeing."

"Will I see these powers, too?"

Tears came to Gazelle's eyes. "You are a brave woman. The powers reveal themselves to whom they please. Maybe you will see them, maybe not. But they will take you."

"Where will I go?"

"It will be a special place, for you faced a lion and death for us."

Bough was fading; she grasped Gazelle's arm. "Tell me more."

"I have heard stories. There will be light, warmth, and stroking. There will be plenty to eat, drink, and much laughter."

"If there is such a place," said Bough, "take my children there."

Gazelle smiled. "It is not their time yet."

"I am ready," said Bough, weakly. "Will you be a mother to my children?"

"Of course. They are one of us now."

A burden lifted from Bough. She breathed easily, if weakly.

"You are one of us, too," added Gazelle, tears flowing from her eyes.

Bough called for her children, who were playing a game with Otter. She managed the strength to hug them and whispered words. Then, she told them to go back to their play.

To Gazelle, she made a request. "Let these two know they are to become *one* when they grow older."

"Are they not brother and sister?" asked Gazelle.

Bough gripped her hand and summoned her strength. She had to say many words, and she did not know if she could.

"Only the boy was born from me ... and from the Elements. The girl came ... from a Hill of Offerings."

Gazelle questioned, "A *Child of the Elements*, and a *Child from the Hill of Offerings*?"

"Are they not good things?"

"The elements bring protection and peril. The Hill of Offerings brings its freedom, but it may still try to claim her. It is good that I know these things."

"She loves wolves," Bough whispered. "She is a sister to Lion Mouth."

"Lion Mouth—who is that?"

There was no answer, for Bough had breathed her last.

Gazelle closed Small One's eyes and wept over the body.

"The Lion Fighter has died," she announced as she rose.

The men were sad, but a burden had been lifted. Bough's children thought she was sleeping.

"It is time to go," said Long Ears. "We must reach the hills before nightfall."

"There is one more thing to do," Gazelle said firmly. "We must take her to a place of power."

Long Ears knew the custom, but objected. "She is not a full New One. It is not required."

"I promised to do this for her! And the children will not understand."

"Then you carry her." Even though they were New Ones, their leaders could be harsh. But Gazelle had promised, so Long Ears allowed her.

She carried Bough for a long way before she became too weak and, stumbling, fell. Otter could not bear to see this anymore, so he carried her.

The New Ones came to a small rocky hill. "This is enough of a high place," said Long Ears. "Is she not a Halfling?"

On the hill an unexpected cave presented its jagged mouth, and near the opening, a large flat rock. Gazelle placed Bough upon the rock.

She stood for a moment. "Yes, I sense Power here in the cave. It is enough."

They each placed a stone near her, so that stones were on all sides of her. Gazelle gave words:

Powers from the Deep Earth! The New Ones give to you the Small One, named Bough. This woman has born a child given to the elements, and saved another from the Hill of Offerings. She did man things to survive, and she fought a lion to save us and her children. Take her to the place where no animals need to be fought, where there will always be food and laughter. I name this cave in memory of the Halfling. It is from her last words, 'Lion Mouth.'

Moments later, the troop heard a distant howl.

"It is time to move on," said Long Ears.

PART II
CHAPTER I
Among the New Ones

At first, the New Ones were hidden among the other groups. Long ago, they had learned to hide themselves, but they could not hide forever. And as they surfaced, they would not have survived, if there had not been Halflings who understood some of their words and ways.

The New Ones changed things, like wearing animal skins. At first, they were mocked for their strange ways. What saved the New Ones was that they were useful. One made a weapon that saved a family from a predator. Another led a group to a cave where water was found.

Bough's children were given new names when they joined the New Ones. The boy had been called Howler, but that did not describe all that he did or felt. When it stormed, he would hold out his hands to receive the rain, and let lightning into his eyes. He stood without fear, and when there was not enough, he would try to make it storm more. And sometimes it seemed he did.

In the rain, the Child of the Elements would think of his mother Bough, how she had fought and protected them, and how a lion killed her. Then his anger would rise, and he would break into a rage.

Knowing these things, the New Ones gave Howler another name. They offered him *Tinder*, to remind him of softness, of what it felt like before the storm. Yet, it was still a true name, for Tinder could erupt.

Bough had saved Wolf Sister as well. She had a way with wolves and could befriend them. The New Ones called her Huntress, for she was helpful in the hunt. A few New Ones had objected, but after days of hunger, she had killed a deer, which fed them for days. "Huntress has luck," they said. "Sometimes, the powers do not see a man or a woman."

Tinder and Huntress squabbled over small things and sometimes came to blows. But they were brother and sister blows. Tinder did not use his full strength and took more hits than he gave.

Even among the New Ones, Tinder and Huntress were different. They had a kind side and treated others in the group as if they were brothers and sisters. Sometimes the New Ones said, "He is Kinder, not Tinder, and she is Carer, not Huntress."

Wolf Sister preferred the name Huntress, for she did not want to be reminded that she cared. Howler had accepted Tinder, for it could explode into fire.

Gazelle wondered how these two could ever be as man and woman. Why had their mother, the Lion Fighter, told her this? How could they be anything but brother and sister? Still, Gazelle decided that she must speak about their mother's wish.

"I have something to tell you about the time before," she began one day.

Tinder and Huntress always wanted to hear more about their mother, and would come together for this.

Gazelle was proud of them. Their bodies were lithe and strong, and it seemed there was nothing they could not do.

"When your mother was dying, after she had fought a great lion...."

"How did she fight the lion?" asked Tinder, as he always did. "There must be more than what you have said."

"Women have hidden strengths," Gazelle replied with a sigh. "She had lion wounds on her back and side, but the lion did not eat her. She told of wolves coming."

Huntress asked, "She fought off wolves too?"

"Maybe the wolves fought the lion?" suggested Tinder

"We know this," Gazelle went on. "She was brave, and she had luck. But her luck ran out. Still, she escaped to us, and her last words were '*Lion Mouth*.' So we named the cave that, where we lay her. Before she died, she had a wish for you both."

They waited, for this was something new.

Gazelle took a breath. "She believed that one day you would be together as a man and woman."

Both Huntress and Tinder protested. "She must mean something else. We are brother and sister."

"Huntress is not from the same mother," Gazelle revealed.

"Who am I from?" asked Huntress.

"You came from the Hill of Offerings."

"I was abandoned?"

Gazelle wondered if she were ready, but it was better that she know now than later. "Yes, you were given to wolves. There must have been reasons. Sometimes, it is to save the group. Sometimes, the parents are too weak to care."

"The wolves did not eat me!"

Huntress explained, "Bough carried you away in time. She became your new mother, and a wolf helped to protect you."

"Why did the wolf not eat us?" asked Huntress.

"It was a young and Bough tamed it. You helped, for you had a gift."

Tinder interjected. "What of me? I know Bough was my mother!"

"Yes, and you have a father whom you do not know and does not know you. So you were given another father. You were given to the Wind and Storm."

"How can the Wind and Storm be my father?" asked Tinder.

"I do not know. But your mother believed that you needed their help. In time, you will find out more what this means."

"If I am given to the Elements, what will they want from me?"

"I do not know."

"We will never be man and woman together," Tinder decided.

Huntress agreed. "How could we ever think such a thing?"

"I have only told you of her wish," Gazelle responded. "She gave you both life."

The boy and girl walked on, going their separate ways.

They are still young, thought Gazelle. *Who knows what the future will bring? Still, it does not seem possible....*

It became even more impossible after a raid by the Fierce Ones.

CHAPTER II

Hyena Land

Fierce Ones would come into their land, seeking to kill them. Day or night, they would swoop down to kill and eat the ones they could take from the group. They would take anyone: man, woman or child. Such was their strength that they fought without sharp sticks.

One day, two Fierce Ones surprised them in the middle of the day. The New Ones held them off, but one of their men died. His body was saved. But as the Fierce Ones retreated, they came upon Huntress, returning with a bird in hand. She was taken.

Tinder raged when he heard. "Where are they? I will find her. I will kill them!"

Gazelle and Otter held him back. "You cannot fight Fierce Ones by yourself! You do not know their strength. And the two that came are likely going back to others."

"I am a *Child of the Elements*. I will fight them with storms and floods! I will take her back!"

Tinder had not spoken his secret name before. Despite that, he knew he was unlikely to succeed. He became silent, seething inside.

"What will happen to her?" asked Tinder.

Gazelle could not bring herself to say.

Tinder saw the answer in Gazelle's face. At that, he left, following the trail.

The Fierce Ones moved fast, but they did not hide their tracks, and Tinder kept pace. The farther away from his own group, the more danger he brought to himself. But his sister had been captured.

The Fierce Ones followed a corridor that went North. To the West was an impassable dry land, and to the east, the Land of Hyenas.

Tinder had an early close call. Another pair of Fierce Ones were searching for more victims. He laid low, and they missed his path.

Tinder pressed on, despite the risk of running into other groups. To his surprise, he came upon Huntress's solitary tracks, heading toward Hyena Land. They were running tracks, spotted with blood. Somehow, she had escaped.

What hope could she have? The hyenas would surely kill her. She had done a bold thing, however. The Fierce Ones would not suspect that path for a woman and would search the drylands.

Tinder knew he must decide what to do. To follow her would bring him into the same danger. But they had always looked out for each other. Had not their mother said they should stay together? It might not be as man and woman, but as brother and sister. He decided he would obey Bough's wish in this way.

Tinder went into a land, eerie and silent. There was no sign of hyenas. He could not believe that Huntress had gone alone into this land, where trees were few and little safety was at hand.

The first night he could not find shelter, so he slept in the open. It was cold, and Tinder went in and out of sleep. A dream came to him that Huntress was surrounded by hyenas and needed help. Tinder sent a storm that lashed around them, and in the confusion, she escaped.

The next morning Tinder lost her track, for the land ahead of him became wet with rain. He paused to consider what Huntress might do. With her tracks erased, she could make a wide arc, double back and return to their group. Or she could go deeper into Hyena Land, where danger was certain and death likely. To go further, with no tracks to follow, would not be wise.

Tinder ranged a distance further out, but there was no sign of any tracks. Then, in the haze, a hyena pack showed on the horizon. He was upwind, but if the wind shifted, it could be his death. Tinder felt he had not much choice but to go back. There was a good chance that Huntress had done the same. Still, he said, "Goodbye sister, if you go ahead." By a sudden impulse, he held out his hands. "I give you the Elements and their protection!"

Why did he think he could place power at a distance? Still, he had done this. Maybe it was from his dream.

Tinder made his way out of Hyena Land, seeing no further trace of Huntress. Randomly searching would only further expose himself, so he took the corridor directly back to the group.

When Tinder arrived, Gazelle was shaken. He saw in her face that Huntress had not returned. His adopted mother hugged him.

Gazelle told about something more that had happened. Two more Fierce Ones had come, but the New Ones had driven them away in the direction Kinder had gone. She had feared that they would chance upon Kinder,

Tinder hardly seemed to hear her. "Could Huntress survive Hyena Land?" he asked.

Gazelle answered carefully. "Huntress has a way with animals. She would find a way ... She is like her mother. She will survive." But inwardly, Gazelle mourned as if she had lost her child.

HUNTRESS HAD SEEN THE speck in the distance, following her. She had thought, *He is just one. I will lie in wait and kill him.* Yet she was wounded, and fear drove her on. She had no sharp stick, and a Fierce One could readily kill her.

Huntress shuddered at the thought of her time with the Fierce Ones. She had screamed and kicked, and it only amused them. She had not known that it was possible for them to be that way.

She called on the Powers when the Fierce Ones had her, but it did not help. She had risen above herself and floated. Seeing the land below, she felt no pain.

Huntress had fought and bit the men. They hit her, and her mind went blank.

When she woke, her head and body were hurting. The dawn had not yet come, and the Fierce Ones were still sleeping. It was a miracle she had escaped. It was only because they thought a woman who had been beaten would not try to flee alone in the wild.

But Huntress ran, without a stick, and without any skins.

At first, she ran as if she was going back home. She knew they would catch up, so she hid her path, turned and went toward Hyena Land. If she could survive a day there, the Fierce Ones might give up. For even they would not readily travel into Hyena Land. With a stone, she killed a lizard and ate it.

Somehow she survived the day. Before it turned dark, Huntress found a lone spindly tree and propped herself high in a fork. Tomorrow, she would circle back. Huntress had thought to carry with her three round stones and a sharpening stone.

Morning came and Huntress was relieved to see no sign of hyenas. She started back, but it was not long before what she feared came to pass. A pack of hyenas was ahead of her, stirring dust. So she fled back into Hyena Land and zigzagged to confuse her track. Huntress became lost in the land.

Still, the pack found her. The next morning—she had found an oak to sleep in—six spotted hyenas were milling below. Their mangy, dark coats were streaked with blood. The pack must have been in a fight recently, with a predator or maybe between themselves. Now they had found easy prey and were in no hurry.

Bough was treed, and even if she made lucky kills with her stones, they would not be enough. She could try to out-wait them, but she sensed the pack had done this before. Their prey would weaken, fall, and they would have their food. Huntress laughed. She, who was Huntress, was hunted.

Huntress had a way with wolves, but not with hyenas. Up close, she saw their look and ways were a mix of wolves and cats, and their raised muscular top half reminded her of bears. She considered fighting while she was still strong. Hyenas were as big as wolves, and if she were lucky, she could kill two or three. But she would die unless something else happened to help her.

Huntress hurled a stone at the hyenas to see if she could wound one and scare the rest. It glanced the side of a hyena who yelped. The group settled a little further out.

Huntress found out that the stones were too small for killing. To go down the tree was death. To wait was death too....

In the heat of the day, the pack forgot the thrown stone and gathered closer to the tree. Then Huntress hurled her largest rock and hit a hyena square on the head. He howled, walked unsteadily, but he was not killed. The group moved out a way again.

Huntress already felt hunger and knew she would grow weak in time. She must make a plan. Her mother, Bough, had always thought of plans. Somehow, she had survived a great lion. *Help me, Bough!* The thought of her mother caused Huntress to stare at the great boughs around her. Something came to her.

With her cutting stone, she spent the rest if the day stripping a tree limb. It was taking time, for the stick must be large and sharp. She had to be careful too, that up in the tree, the stick would not fall from her hands.

The hyenas watched and shifted uneasily. Somehow they knew she was making a weapon. Huntress finished sharpening the branch and realized that her thirst had become fierce. With her cutting stone, she cut at the tree and tasted its bitter sap.

Huntress formed a plan. With the pointed stick, she would kill a hyena. Then the others would eat him and be satisfied. She would do it tomorrow, in the heat of the day when the hyenas drew close.

At night Huntress's mind wandered, and she thought of Tinder. Why did they fight all the time? She had known him since she could remember, and wasn't he her best friend? He helped her when she needed help. And no man bothered her, for Tinder could become fierce.

Morning came, and the hyenas were out of range. By midday, faint rolls of thunder sounded, and it rained. Huntress licked the leaves and opened her mouth in the rain. Her thirst eased. When the thunder grew louder and lightning flashed, the hyenas came under the tree, forgetting about her.

She aimed the stick. Her vision seemed to waver, but her hand held steady. She was Huntress. She threw the stick and struck a hyena in the back, drawing blood. The entire pack howled as one fierce howl.

But the hyena shrugged off the wound and still walked. Huntress had lost, and the hyenas had won. But Huntress was determined. *No, they will not have me!* She propped herself in a fork of a tree, so she would not fall. A leopard would likely have her in time, but not the hyenas. She fell asleep, wandering if she would wake.

CHAPTER III

Wolf People

Huntress dozed on and off, her dreams feverish. Hunger and thirst had caught up to her. The hyenas became impatient, for they smelled death. Vultures winged above, and Huntress realized that the great birds would eat her before a leopard would come.

She woke to a sharp flash of pain. A bird's beak had probed her leg. Huntress struck with her sharpening stone and hit the bird square in the breast. The stunned vulture fell from the tree, and the hyenas leapt upon it. That changed everything. After they devoured the great bird, the pack left.

Huntress had survived the hyenas, but she was too weak to climb down. She would die, but at least she was safe a while longer.

It surprised her to wake to brightness with her back flat on the ground. Was she in the land that Gazelle had spoken of? Huntress looked up and saw a wolf staring down at her. A person was on the wolf's side. Yes, this was a strange land, like a dream.

The Wolf People had found her. They had come upon the tree and their wolves had scented her. Surprised to find her alive, they carried her down.

Huntress was too weak to speak, but she heard voices.

"It is a good sign. The wolves lay by her."

"The hyenas had her surrounded, but she did not die. See, she drew blood with her stick."

"She is like us, a Wolf Woman. Bring her skins to wear."

Huntress could not believe her luck. She had come under the protection of a group whose animal was wolf. They were some dozen strong. An older woman with gray hair tended to her, giving her water and food to eat. She did not speak much, except to say a few soothing words.

Huntress sensed something was different about this group. They were not *New Ones*, but she wondered if they were Halflings. The Wolf People were willing to wait until she was well enough to travel and set up camp around the tree.

She found herself part of a smaller group: the silent older one, and a Small One who seemed to have no parents. This girl looked as if no one had trained her to do things, for she did nothing useful. She stayed by Huntress's side and played with flowers she had found.

"What is your name?" Huntress asked.

The girl looked down shyly.

"Has no one given you a name yet? You have given me flowers, so I will call you *Giving Flower*. That will be your name between us."

After a few hours of rest, Huntress regained her strength. The Wolf People seemed not to fear the hyenas and continued straight through the land. They were led by a man named Gray Eyes, who decided things with both wisdom and firmness. Once, a pack of hyenas tested them. The Wolf People made a circle with their sticks pointed out, stomped the ground, and shouted. Their own wolves snarled. They and the wolves acted like one great beast, and the hyena pack left.

Huntress thought of Tinder and Gazelle, and how they would think she was dead. Holding her hands high, she sent a cry to them. She sent wolf power, saying, "*I do not see you, but let good wolves be with you!*"

The next day, something happened which made her know how different Wolf People were. The Small One, whom Huntress had secretly named, became hurt late in the day. She had fallen, broken her leg and could not walk.

It did not seem like a big break, and it was in the lower leg. There was no bone jutting out. Yet the leg was swollen and there would be too much pain for the child to walk. Huntress remembered that this had happened in her travels before, and that the girl could be healed. But it would take time. The Wolf People set up camp for the night.

That evening Huntress was surprised to learn that the group had decided to leave Small One behind. They set her apart from the group and gave her no food. She cried from hunger and being alone, so Huntress went over to her. "Is there no one to care for you? I will share my food with you." She began stroking the girl until Gray Eyes came over.

"Leave her alone," he ordered.

When Huntress did not move, Gray Eyes shared more words to explain the ways of his people. "Why speak to one who is going to die? Her lameness brings danger to all of us. If the hyenas see a lame one, they will follow us until we give her up. It is better to leave her behind now. It is a rule we follow in passing through this land."

Huntress looked into the eyes of the man and saw he was a Halfling, one who could listen and be moved by words.

"Does she not have a male to protect her?"

Gray Eyes wondered at the question, but he answered. "Her mother and father have died."

To Gray Eye's surprise, Huntress kept speaking. "Among our people, we care for hurt ones like this. She will be well enough to walk in a day or two."

"In Hyena Land? We are fierce when we need to be, but we are not foolish. We have already delayed for you. And hyenas are not all that is here. A large cat can become attracted to her weakness as well."

Gray Eyes read her face and sensed her determination, but it did not change his mind. "We must leave this un-named one behind. In the morning you will come with us."

Huntress saw that Gray Eyes had decided and said no more. She had wanted to say that she had given the name "Giving Flower." But Huntress was not fully part of the group, and her words would not carry much weight.

Huntress realized she was not free. She couldn't leave the group and survive alone. What could she do? The Wolf People had saved her. Not all people were like the New Ones....

Huntress gazed at the Small One, who was half grown, and to whom she had given a name. Giving Flower did not fully know what was happening, yet sensed something was wrong. She clung to Huntress's legs and would not let go. Somehow, she knew that her life depended on this newcomer. But what could Huntress do? She pulled away, in spite of the girl's sobs, and felt torn inside.

The wolves caught rabbits, and all ate except the lame one. That night, Huntress only ate part of her food. She stroked the wolf, who was her friend, and gave him some food.

When the Small One wailed from hunger and pain, one of the Wolf People buffeted her. Huntress wanted to attack the man, but she held herself back. She looked around to see if others were pained. The other women didn't seem to care. Only the Silent One's eyes revealed more.

If Huntress were a man, she would have the strength to help the girl. *If only Tinder were here. He could challenge Gray Eyes and fight to save this Small One.*

Huntress was wondering whether to bring food to the girl, when the image came to her of something her mother had once done. Bough had fashioned a small stick to mend a bird's leg, and the bird was able to fly away.

Huntress cut a stick, something she knew well how to do. The Wolf People watched curiously, for their women did not do such things. Then she wove grass together in a rope and went to the Lame One.

The Wolf People watched and wondered. Some thought she would kill the Lame One. But Healer placed the stick against the leg and wrapped the woven grass around the leg and stick.

Gray Eyes was curious. "What have you done?"

"I have given her leg the strength of a stick to help her walk."

Gray Eyes considered this. He had not seen this, yet it might work. He knew that other people had their own knowledge. "How can a stick give strength to a leg?" he asked.

Huntress did not know the answer, but said, "My mother did this with hurt animals, and they walked again." It was a lie. She had only seen Bough do it once with a bird, but the man did not notice the lie. He saw what she had done, and it looked like she had done it before.

Gray Eyes shrugged. "If she can walk, she can come." He stepped away, then turned and said, "You are more than a Huntress, if you can fix bent legs."

"I am Huntress," she answered, not wanting to reveal other names. "The Small One will have to have strength. I have saved Giving Flower some food."

The eyes of the wolf leader flashed with anger. "You have named her?" But he allowed Huntress to wrap the bough around her leg. Maybe this woman could save a male hunter this way.

"Why did you name her?" he asked.

"She stayed by my side when I could not move. I had nothing else to give."

This made sense to Gray Eyes. "You had cause to gift her." Gray Eyes searched Huntress, as if trying to find this other name for her.

He nodded. "You may feed her as well. She will need strength." When some protested with taunting laughs, Gray Eyes quieted them with a look.

Huntress could not believe she had gained a male ally, if only in part. Still, the Lame One must walk in the morning––one who looked weak and like she could not take much pain.

Huntress's mother had called her Healer once, and she felt the name rising in her. *I must not look with the eyes, nor work with the hands of a Hunter now.*

Healer fed the Lame One, and the others watched. "They call her Huntress, but she would heal and defend one she hardly knows."

"She is not your child," one man told her. "You are not Healer."

"When one is sick and alone, one becomes your child," Huntress replied.

The men did not understand, but they did not stop her. The women did not anger, neither did they seem to care.

Night fell, and Healer stayed with the girl.

Giving Flower clutched her hand throughout the night, her face holding fear even when she slept.

"You must walk when the sun comes. The bough will give you strength," Healer explained.

"Do not leave me," asked the Small One, whose words were rare.

"I will be with you, but you must walk by my side."

"Mother?" asked the child.

Huntress almost said she was not. But Healer saw the Small One's pain and her hope and remembered her own story. Did not the first mother she knew find her abandoned on a Hill of Offerings? How could she not be mother to one like herself?

"Yes, I am," she finally answered.

That night the child slept fitfully and moaned when she shifted. "Do not think of the pain," directed Healer. "Think of beautiful things, like the sky and clouds. Think of playing in the sun, near gentle waters and flowers." Giving Flower quieted, but Huntress herself could hardly sleep. She had gained a child, but did not know if her child would survive the next day.

Huntress got up restless. She went over to the wolves, stroked, and talked to the one who liked her. The wolf looked into Huntress's eyes and saw that she knew him.

Then Huntress returned to her child, lowered her head, and tears came.

The others slept, but Gray Eyes noticed. *Has she another name?* he thought, wondering about this woman.

The dawn sky was flaming red. Healer did not know if this was a good sign. It could mean that blood would be spilled, or it could mean new life. It gave them some time, as the group milled about, looking.

Healer helped the Small One to her feet. She yelped and winced. "Do not think of the pain," said Healer. "I will stay by your side and help you."

The troop was readying to leave when Gray Eyes came over. Healer was propping the girl up, readying to help her walk.

"The Small One must walk on her own. No lame ones."

The girl, with panic in her eyes, clutched Healer.

"Walk and live," said Healer. "You must walk on your own. Think of the flowers in the fields and the birds hopping about. You are Giving Flower."

Healer let her go, and she stood.

The child tried to walk and fell. Huntress reached out an arm, steadying her. Sensing harsh stares, she withdrew her arm and said, "Walk and live."

Giving Flower walked. There were tears down her face from the pain. Healer sang as she had heard her mother making rhymes when she was small.

The Wolf People thought her strange, making baby talk to a half-grown one. But Healer did not care. Their leg was not in pain. Song would help her child to survive. When the group stopped to rest,

Giving Flower called out for more singing. It was the thread carrying her life. But Healer knew that it would not be for long.

Gray Eyes listened. This was more than baby or bird talk. It was a flow of words that made one float and forget. *Who is this woman?* he asked himself again. *Each thing she does is a surprise.*

It was slowing the group, but Gray Eyes allowed the slowness. Besides, there were no hyenas on their trail, and they would be out of Hyena Land soon enough. He had decided too that Huntress was of value and could become a full member of their group. If one of his men got hurt, maybe she could heal him. Gray Eyes could think of the future. Huntress could help the group survive. Gray Eyes fished about for her name, but Healer clung to it.

Giving Flower walked and made it to the next place of rest. Her pain, however, had increased, and her leg had swollen. Healer realized that Small One could not walk by herself anymore. She had failed, despite her efforts. The Healer in her knew this would take more time.

When the group rose, Healer helped up the girl. The Small One leaned on her, clutching fiercely with an arm. If Healer let her go, she would fall and not be able to get up again.

So Healer walked with Giving Flower, helping to steady her.

At first, no one noticed. Then someone spoke out, "She is lame! She cannot walk!"

Gray Eyes came over and said, "Let her go."

"No," said Healer, looking squarely at him.

Gray Eyes struck her face. Huntress clinched her fists and looked back fiercely. Healer did nothing more, for it would do no good to fight. She might wound Gray Eyes, even get help from her wolf friend. But the wolf was just one and might not answer her. She wondered why she was standing up in this way. For now, it was likely that both she and the Small One would be struck down.

Gray Eyes could not believe that Huntress was defiant. No woman from another group could be allowed to challenge him. He struck her on the leg with his stick, a sharp blow. It was not so sharp as to break her leg, but enough for her to cry out in pain.

Huntress stopped her cry short. She must not show weakness, even though she could not fight. She returned to her fierce look. It puzzled Gray Eyes. Her wolf friend had come closer to her, wondering what was happening.

A faint trembling came over Huntress's body, and she could not stop it. She was afraid. "Let her go," ordered Gray Eyes for the last time, and he raised his stick to strike.

CHAPTER IV

Kinder's Dream

Huntress raised her hand and cried out, "I cannot let go. My name is Healer. I must help the Lame One."

Gray Eyes paused; his stick still raised. A woman who had the name Healer would help his group survive. But she had defied him. It should not have come to this....

Then the Silent One spoke. "Gray Eyes! Can you not see she is a *New One?* She defends the child not to challenge you. With the name Healer, she has no choice but to live her name. She is bonded to anyone she has named, as if it were her own child, even if it be a Small One."

Healer suddenly realized that this woman must be a New One too. Would her words be enough to save her?

The Wolf People listened, for in times before, even when they had not wanted to hear her, what she said had turned out to be true. Her words carried weight, and she knew the wisdom of names.

Gray Eyes lowered his stick and drew a step closer to Huntress, as if to see her better. *Could she be a Woman of Power, something only the Silent One saw? To kill such a one, even if she were from another land, would not be a good thing. And the Silent One had spoken for her.* But the leader had been challenged and he could not let that stand, for the group's life depended on them following his word.

At that point, yet another in the group rose to Healer's defense. The wolf, whom she had befriended, came to her side and issued a low growl.

Gray Eyes held up, surprised. The tension broke. The men laughed. "She has a male friend! Would Gray Eyes fight one who has such a strong male to defend her?"

The leader lowered his stick. He had his way out. He could back down before a wolf defender, although he knew this wolf would obey him, that his growl was more questioning than anything else.

Gray Eyes looked around and saw the New Ones gave this woman a begrudging respect. Healer had not run from pain and had taken blows for a girl child, one of their own.

The Wolf clan leader stepped away, wondering about what had happened. This woman was a Healer and likely a New One. She had befriended a wolf and defended one of theirs as her child. How many names did this woman have?

The next day Huntress journeyed with the Wolf People into a new land. They met a wide, swift, and winding river. On the other side, a rocky and barren land was said to be filled with snakes, and no one would venture there.

Huntress had little choice but to go with the Wolf People. She could not cross Hyena Land alone. At least she was safe for now. Maybe they would come near her land again. Her wolf friend walked with her. *With a wolf, I might have a chance,* she thought.

THINGS HAD CHANGED for the New Ones, for their numbers had grown as smaller groups of New Ones joined them. The *Child of the Elements* did not cry for Wolf Sister anymore, but he would rage. Seeing his grief, the others learned not to bother him.

To make matters worse, it was at the time that Tinder should make his first kill and become a full hunter. The first kill could not be a smaller animal like a lone jackal or a wildcat, but a dangerous kill, like a wolf, a hyena, or even a young bear. Tinder had no luck. The animals seemed to know he was there before he approached, and they escaped.

"It will take time," said Long Ears.

Tinder did not care. *What does it matter when my sister is lost, and I cannot find her?* He held his grief silently.

Gazelle tried to comfort him. "Maybe she lives. She escaped from the Fierce Ones."

"How many days can one survive alone in Hyena Land?" asked Tinder. "And if she survived, she has found another group. How will they treat her? How long will they let her live?"

Gazelle did not have answers. "Maybe she has the luck of her mother."

"I have sent her power," Tinder revealed.

Gazelle was surprised, for she had not heard him speak of his power in this way before. "What did you send her?"

"The power of storm––lightning and thunder."

Gazelle laughed gently, but she saw the seriousness in Tinder's eyes. *Could he have the Power of Storm?* she wondered. True, he did not fear thunder or lightning, for he would go out in the middle of storms. But had he ever called upon one? Yet, he had tried to give this power to his sister.

"Do you love her?" she asked one day.

He answered with a sudden fierceness. "I am a *Child of the Elements*! I am Howler, and I am Tinder. I am not one who loves."

"Did you not go into Hyena Land to find her?"

"I left her there, too."

"With no tracks, what else could you have done? Do you not grieve her now?"

The *Child of the Elements* lowered his head. It was true. "She is my sister," he explained.

Gazelle persisted, for she remembered Bough's words. "You have yet another name other than Howler, Tinder, and *Child of the Elements*. It is Kinder."

Tinder looked back fiercely. "I do not have this name! I will not take it!"

Gazelle said softly, "I am your mother now. Can I not name what I see?"

"Bough was my mother!"

"She gave you to me."

It was true. It was the wish of his mother. Tinder was confused, for he was not ready for a new name. If he took this name, his feelings would come out in a flood--how much he cared for Huntress, and how he could not bear her loss.

Gazelle understood. "You need not accept the name now."

The *Child of the Elements* changed his mind. "I do not fear this name. If it will bring Huntress back, I will be Kinder."

Gazelle sighed. "Maybe one day she will come back. Let us call her again."

They had done this before. Gazelle held Kinder's hand in hers, and they raised their hands up. "Think of her and wish her home."

They stood together, their hands raised toward Hyena Land. "Come home, Huntress! Come to us!"

Days passed and Huntress did not come.

Kinder asked why their calls had not worked.

"The calls have power," Gazelle answered. "At least, she will know that we are calling her and that we await her."

One night, Kinder saw Huntress in a dream. She was living among wolves who talked. They did not eat her, but she was captive.

Kinder told Gazelle about his dream.

"You remembered your dream? The New Ones have this gift, dreams that can see at a distance. The calling has worked, for you have seen her a dream."

"What does it mean?" asked Kinder.

"Huntress is alive and protected by wolves. But she is not happy and wishes to be among her own."

"Then we must find her and bring her home."

Gazelle did not answer. There were too few New Ones to risk passage through Hyena Land.

"She was caring for a small wolf," Kinder suddenly remembered.

Gazelle considered for a moment. "It means——maybe she has a child."

"A child!" Emotions went through Kinder. "She has a male protector, too?"

"She would need protection to survive in a group. But we do not know what has happened. It is still a dream that may or may not be."

"When I am a full man, I will find her," Kinder declared. "I will bring her home. I will free my sister from the wolves!"

Gazelle did not think it possible. She asked, "Is that all that was in the dream?"

Kinder had held back one thing. "There was a fight between wolves and bears. There was blood and death. Afterwards, only a small girl and a baby survived. I was looking at this from afar. What does it mean?"

Gazelle's face lined with worry. "I am not sure. There may be a battle in the future.... But let go of the dream for now. It is time to gather food."

Kinder obeyed, but his dream did not leave him. Although there were more questions than answers, he had hope. Huntress was still alive.

Kinder secretly readied for a journey. He spent more time with the men to learn their ways. The New Ones joked and called him the son of many fathers. Kinder also studied the ways of bears.

"Are you searching for a new name?" asked Gazelle.

Kinder was silent, for others would surely not approve.

Still, the men warned him. "You cannot predict the ways of a bear. It is easier to kill a wolf than a bear."

Gazelle saw that Kinder was determined. "You are ready to become a full hunter. Yet, you must be careful. You did not have a father to teach you when you were young."

Tinder spoke. "I have a father; I am a *Child of the Elements*! I can make friends with a bear if I want!"

Gazelle wondered, *Can Kinder really tame a bear? Who knows the power of a name, if one is true to it. His mother had made friends with a wolf. But a bear?*

One day, Kinder brought two bear cubs to camp. They were tame enough, yet it worried the New Ones. "Where is the mother bear? Will not the bears grow and change? One does not know what a bear will do. The New Ones have befriended animals before, but a bear is something else."

Kinder said the mother bear had died, and that young bears could learn their ways.

Gazelle defended Kinder. "This new thing has happened for a reason. Maybe the bears will bring us power. Maybe it is the will of Bough, who died and gave her life for the *New Ones*."

When the name of Bough was mentioned, the *New Ones* listened.

Gray Eyes decided. "We will honor his mother, even if her son has not made his first kill. And we will watch these two bears closely."

For part of the year, the *New Ones* would move to a lake-side where there would be more game. They did not have to pass through Hyena Land, but there were always dangers in travel.

Kinder wanted to bring his bears, who had grown to half a man's size.

"The bears are not part of our group," said one man.

"They will not fight us," Kinder assured.

Gazelle spoke on Kinder's behalf. "If the boy-man has no fear, why should we?"

What could the hunting men say to this? If one spoke for someone else and there was no answer, it would stand. They were not like others, whose leaders decided things no matter which way the words went.

Still, Gray Eyes said, "One bear can come, but not two."

So Kinder set the female bear free to roam. It was difficult, but he left her at the place where she had been found.

The *New Ones* made their passage to the lake. At the start, they had to fend off a lone leopard. They succeeded, for they had a dozen experienced men.

For days there was no sign of any other large animal. Yet they remained alert, for they were leaving tracks behind, and no rain had hidden them.

The troop was searching for a safe place to rest when danger came. A pack of wolves had scented them. At first they were a few, then they howled, summoning two dozen more.

The New Ones knew that a time of testing had come. It was bad luck for such a large pack to find them. All would have to fight who could––men, women, young and old. Everyone readied their sticks and picked up rocks. They had a bit of good fortune. They had come to a small rise whose ground bore stones.

Kinder's bear's hair raised, sensing danger. There was just time to form a circle before they were surrounded.

The wolves attacked at once, but the circle held. Kinder had placed the bear in the middle, where young girls held babies. It was a last line of defense if one broke through.

Again and again, the wolves came from all sides. They were trying to wound or kill, and drag someone away. Many of the New Ones gained bite marks, but none fell. The wolves fought fiercely. Then one wolf was killed and a second seriously wounded.

The pack drew back and howled. But it would not be long before the fight resumed.

"We will all die unless we do something!" cried one man.

Gray Eyes had no answer, except to say, "We must fight for our young."

Gazelle looked about and saw Kinder, whose arms were wounded and whose eyes had a fierce glaze. "Are you not a *Child of the Elements*?" she asked. "Why have you not called on the Powers?"

Kinder looked up at the sky, which held clouds. He had not summoned a storm in some time, but he raised his hands and cried out:

> *Come Storm and Thunder,*
> *Rain and Fire!*
> *Scatter the fierce beasts!*

Some New Ones thought this was craziness, but they did not object, for it might save them.

Nothing happened right away. But the clouds gathered and darkened, as they would in the late afternoon.

The wolves resumed their attack. They were too many, and the New One's line weakened. One man was killed. Then the wolves dashed through the circle and killed a baby. As they pulled away, the male bear attacked. It lunged at a wolf and buffeted him senseless to the ground with a single blow.

Five wolves approached the bear.

"Draw back," cried Long Ears. "Let the bear fight!"

CHAPTER V

Challenge of Huntress

The men and women picked up their children and withdrew.

The bear stood its ground. *This was the plan,* Kinder realized. *The wolves would have the dead man, the baby, and the bear. Then the New Ones could escape!*

"I will not leave the bear!" cried Kinder.

Gazelle grabbed his arm. "The bear fights for us. The New Ones must live."

Kinder sensed rain in the darkened sky, but not a storm. He fled with the New Ones.

They had gained time, but the wolves would not be satisfied. The New Ones must soon find a safe place, but would the land offer one?

They ran. There was only flat land before them, and the wolves would catch up to them. "Run, run!" the men cried.

It started to rain, a soft drizzle.

The New Ones stopped, out of breath and exhausted.

"Call the rain again!" cried Gazelle. "Call the rain!"

The *Child of the Elements* raised his hands and called upon the storm. Neither thunder nor lightning came, but the rain became a downpour, enough to wash the land.

The New Ones laughed and ran through the rain, for it was covering their tracks. They must run through the rain as far as they could.

They heard the pack's howls in the distance. The bear had finally died and would become food for the wolves. But the New Ones had reached a rocky area near the lake, a safe place to tend their wounds.

There was much happiness, and talk of the bear and Kinder, and how the New Ones had survived. That night the clan made Kinder a full hunter. Everyone laughed for happiness. Kinder had not made his first kill, but he had tamed a bear that fought for them, had he not? The bear had fought in the boy's place, killed wolves and saved many lives.

One hunter raised a protest, but there was no stopping the words. If there was any doubt remaining, Gray Eyes ended it, saying: "There is more to Kinder's help than his bear fighting for us. Kinder called rain, and it gave us life. He is a full hunter now. He is a Bear Tamer and a Rain Caller."

To be given a new name, when he had not made his first major kill, seemed strange to Kinder. Yet he had been given two. Kinder wondered if he should accept this. Yet how could he refuse? Had he not tamed the bear? Had he not drawn the rain, or was that chance? Kinder decided it did not matter how. The New Ones had survived, and he had two new names.

The clan celebrated, and for a time Kinder forgot his grief from losing his sister and his bear. He was a full hunter now, and he could leave on his own. He would find his sister.

HUNTRESS SENSED THINGS were changing. The Wolf People had to range further to find food. And something worse than hunger had come. A group of Fierce Ones had been sighted in their land. Would they not have to fight them one day if they stayed? Huntress shuddered at the thought and began to have terrible dreams.

One day Gray Eyes died; he did not wake from his sleep. A new leader of the clan emerged, a younger man named Flint. He was not a Halfling or a New One. These were hard times, and Flint was a hard man. He knew the rules of survival, and he stuck to the rules. It was time for the Wolf People to move on and see if they could find a new place.

Huntress wondered what it meant for her, for she had some protection with Gray Eyes. He had understood her, even though he had struck her. Things were changing.

Giving Flower was grown now, and Huntress could teach her a few things. The Small One never learned to trap animals, but she remembered plants and could collect them. She liked to hold babies, and she still gave flowers. Huntress loved her.

Sometimes, Huntress longed to return to her old home. But she would say to herself that she had a child now whom she must protect.

One day as they walked, Flint, who hardly talked to Huntress, asked, "This Giver of Flowers does not help the group much. What good does she do?"

"She makes me happy, and she helps me find plants. She is my child. Do I not provide enough food for her and more?"

It was true. Huntress was a good hunter. When no one else could find something, she could find a rabbit or a bird.

Still, Flint pursued, "Why do you not have your own child? The Wolf People need more young."

Huntress had no response.

"You need a man," Flint decided. "I could defend you."

"I have a male from the land I come from," Huntress revealed.

"How can one so far away be your man?"

"He is no ordinary man. He is a *Child of the Elements,* and I am his."

Flint did not believe her, for she had been with them for some time. "If you had such a man, he would have come for you."

Gazelle could only say, "He will."

"Why does he wait?"

Gazelle had no answer.

Flint had won the words, but he was not sure. He knew that Huntress was an unusual woman. Maybe she knew a Man of Power. Maybe, too, they would one day go near the place where he was. He had heard of children born with Powers so that wind and water would obey. He did not think it was so, yet how could he be sure?

Flint held off. "By the next full moon your man must come, or you will find one among the Wolf People."

"He will come," said Huntress, with defiance in her voice.

Flint was not happy at being delayed. "Your Flower Child is a burden. But if a man defends you, what can I say?"

Flint left. He was a hard man. Yet he had spoken about what others thought.

Huntress cried. If only Tinder would come.

Not long after this, the Wolf People encountered two stragglers: an older man and a boy about to become a man. They told how they had survived the Fierce Ones. The Wolf People took them in, even though the man was old.

That night Flint suggested to Huntress, "If you will not have one of us, how about one of these. Maybe the young one for the Small One and the old man for you?"

Flint laughed and Huntress wondered if she would be forced to take the old man. He had looked at her.

Huntress felt desperate. Where was Tinder? She could not run away, yet it was getting harder to stay.

Giving Flower sensed danger and clung tightly. Huntress reassured her, "You are my child, and I will protect you."

The Wolf Clan continued their journey into a scrubland, which held small burrowing animals. They found just enough to eat, although they often resorted to insects and larvae.

When the full moon arrived, Huntress had not yet taken a man. Flint remembered and came to her two days later. In front of others, he addressed her, "You have not yet taken a man. I will not force you to do so now. But it is time to leave the Slow One behind. We have grown too hungry to share with one who cannot help the group."

"No!" Huntress refused. "She is a Wolf Person too!"

Flint angered at this challenge. He immediately swung at Huntress, but she leapt back.

"I have a right to challenge, to fight with sticks," she declared, raising hers.

Flint was surprised; he had expected a blow would settle things. "This is how things are decided between men."

"I am Huntress. I have killed animals and am like a man."

Flint wavered between laughter and anger. "No woman challenges a man and lives." He lunged with his stick, feinting a blow at her head, then swung the stick low and tripped her.

Huntress rolled, going far to avoid the next blow that slammed down. The stick caught her hand, and it blazed with pain. She howled, half in pain and half in a cry to her wolf friend. Huntress got up and stepped back. The wolf did not come, for the other men held him back.

Huntress had never fought a man before. Flint was strong and fast, and she would not likely survive. She needed Tinder now, but he was not here. It had been foolish not to befriend a man. She parried the next few blows, but then her stick was hit so hard that it brought pain down the length of her arm. She could think of only one thing to do, a fighting trick. There would be one chance. She would die, but she might stop this man.

Before she could act, Flint thrust at her head. Huntress blocked the stick, pushing it down to the side. But it cut her, and she was exposed for a second blow. Flint did not immediately strike again. He had stopped, not wanting to kill a woman.

Huntress drew back as if retreating, and the man charged. She threw her stick at him. It was something the Wolf People did not do--her secret way of hunting.

Flint was surprised, for the thrown spear grazed his thigh, drawing blood. He howled, picked up both sticks, and started toward her. He would have to kill her now.

CHAPTER VI

Passage

Huntress had only words to defend herself. "Do not touch me! I am the child of a woman who faced a great lion. I have no fear of dying. But do you think you can kill me without having the Powers avenge me? My man is a *Child of the Elements* and he will come for you too!" She let loose his name of power, and it had an effect.

Flint slowed; he had heard of such stories. But they were stories. He laughed and continued on.

Then something happened that no one foresaw. One of the stragglers, who had just joined their group, stepped forward. "Is this not enough? The Fierce Ones are coming! Why kill this woman when danger nears us? Do we not need all of our hunters? Did she not just throw a stick and draw blood against a male hunter? True, she has no child of her own. She is named Huntress. She does not go with men, for she kills animals."

Flint gripped his stick hard and glared. "Who are you, Old Man, to challenge me?"

Huntress wondered how this man could have any hope of winning against a much younger man. She gained a faint hope, however.

Flint considered, he could take on an old man and win. Still, it was not good to fight another man if there was no need. And this Old One did not have a woman and might take this one.

Flint called out to Huntress. "Will you take him as your man?"

Huntress was frozen, unable to speak.

Flint turned to the older man. "Will you protect this silent woman, who will not say she is yours?"

To everyone's surprise, he answered, "Yes."

Flint laughed. "You will protect a woman who does not accept you? Will she not fight you next? You are crazy, old man."

Flint wheeled his stick toward the man.

The Old Man quickly steeled, raising his stick. It was sharp and hardened with fire.

Flint paused before striking, studying the man. He could win, but the man's stick looked as if it had drawn many wounds. And had he not just survived the Fierce Ones? Would he not be needed later? Still, the other men wondered why their leader was not fighting now.

Huntress realized their lives hung by a thread and gathered the Small One in her arms.

Flint had offered a way out, but he was unhappy with the old man's challenge. He decided to probe to see if the old man had strength. Maybe it was bluff, maybe not. If the man was weak, it would not hurt to kill him.

Flint swung his stick, but the blow was solidly blocked. Blow was matched for blow. In time Flint could wear him out, but the old man was good. Once, it seemed the old man could have struck him, but did not. Could it be that he had held back?

Flint stopped fighting. "You are her man. She is yours, even if she does not accept you."

The old man accepted. "I will protect her and her child."

Huntress had tears in her eyes when the old man came over. How could she refuse one who had risked his life for her? She had been saved by an old lion.

The man saw her fear. "I am not looking for a woman. Cover your wound." He handed her a skin.

Huntress didn't know what to think, but the man's eyes looked true. "What is your name? Why have you defended me?"

The man had not often been asked his name, and he rarely gave it after a first meeting. It was bold, but this woman was bold. So he answered her, "My name is Sharpener."

Huntress looked at the man and asked again with her eyes.

"I am not looking for a woman," he repeated. "You were willing to die for your child, and you needed a male defender. No other rose, so I did."

"She is not a child from my body," Huntress revealed. "But I have become like her mother."

"You are even more mother to her, for you were willing to give your life for an unclaimed one. Tell me, why did you throw your stick and leave yourself defenseless?"

"I have killed animals this way."

Sharpener felt the top of her spear. "Your stick is sharp. How did you learn how to do this?"

"My mother taught me such things, but she has died. She fought a great lion too!"

The Sharpener nodded. "You must be a New One to do such things. And you have courage like your mother."

"You know of the New Ones?"

"When one is old, one knows many things."

Huntress wondered. "I must give you something for saving me and my child, but I have nothing to give you."

"You can give me something. At night, tell me stories about yourself and your mother."

Huntress knew that, as people grew older, they liked tales. Yet she wondered if this would be enough.

Two nights later, Huntress, the Small One, and the old man were around the fire.

"Tell me," asked Sharpener. "Where you came from and what your mother was like? What was her name?"

Huntress did not want to give her mother's name so easily, yet the man had already given his and had risked his life for her. How could she refuse?

"She was called Bough and sometimes the Trembling One. She became my mother because she found me."

The man waited, his eyes seeing her deeply. Huntress told the story of how she had befriended a wolf and how the wolf had helped them survive.

The old man surprised her when he spoke. "I have heard of a Trembling One, and that she had a boy child. Do you know what became of him?"

Huntress's amazement grew. "I did not tell you this. How did you know?"

"I have wandered far. Is the boy alive?"

"I know he lives. But we have been apart for some time now. Howler lives with New Ones on the other side of Hyena Land."

The man looked afar and asked in a quiet voice, "And what of his father?"

"His father wandered and did not return. He must have died. But the boy has a new father now."

The man's eyes raised in surprise. "How can that be?"

"Since his mother had no male to protect him, she gave him to the Elements. After that, she found me on a Hill of Offerings and saved me from wolves."

"She carried two babies?"

"Bough was strong and fierce. She fought off animals. We helped her when we grew old enough." Huntress showed scars on her arms and legs.

The man turned away. "Enough. It is time for sleep."

Huntress lay down, not believing she had survived, and that a man favored her with little demand. It was luck, and she wondered how long it would last. But why worry about the day when luck would turn? So far, she had survived.

WHEN THE *New Ones* returned to their usual home, Kinder resolved to make passage across Hyena Land and find Huntress. He had grown strong and had learned more from the men about the ways of the hunt. Finally, he had killed a dangerous predator, a lynx. Kinder also found the female bear that he had set free. For him, she was still tame, and he would stay with her on the camp's outskirts.

It seemed the New Ones had become as restless as him. Food was hard to find, so the male hunters had to range further out. There was talk of finding a new place. Maybe they would cross Hyena Land, and Kinder would not have to travel alone. Yet it was held to be too dangerous, and what the land beyond would offer was unknown.

Kinder wondered how he would survive the crossing, if the group felt it could not. The female bear would journey with him, but would it be enough? He would wait until she grew larger.

Gazelle saw his restlessness and sensed his plan. How could she stop him? Was it not the will of his mother that he be with her?

"There is a way across, I have heard," she told him one day. "If you travel fast all night for two nights, you will see dawn in another land. Will your bear run with you?"

"She will. And we will be leaving soon."

"I know," said Gazelle, her face betraying anxiety. "Do not forget your own kind. Survive!"

"I am a *Child of the Elements*. I will be protected."

"Yes," said Gazelle, with tears in her eyes.

Kinder thought of his dream of the fight between the bears and wolves. *It will be dangerous, but I will survive!*

Kinder and the bear left at twilight. In Hyena Land the bear loped easily, following him. She was nearly full grown and larger than him.

Kinder had planned for the journey. Traveling by night was not what a bear would normally do. But he had taken the bear on night walks, and she became used to it. Toward the end of his preparation, he would run, and the bear would run with him.

When they first entered Hyena Land, the bear was not sure. She looked at him as if to question. But Kinder pressed on, and the bear followed.

The first day there were no sightings of hyenas. Twice, the bear's hairs rose, and she lifted her nose to the air. Then Kinder would change direction and make a wide arc. Once, he passed several human skulls with teeth holes in them.

Another time he saw hyena skeletons among the markings of a camp. It could only be Fierce Ones who had killed so many hyenas. Kinder kept running, his sides hurting.

He remembered a story of the people who had once lived in this land. They were not Fierce Ones, but people who knew the ways of wolves.

They were lucky, for they survived a day of sleep in the open land. Perhaps the hyenas avoided the bear's scent, for it was not their usual prey.

Kinder ran for the second night, and the bear ran with him. Nearly across the land, he became exhausted and started walking. In the twilight, two straggler hyenas eyed him and made a high-pitched whine. But after seeing the bear, their manes retracted, and they did not attack.

Kinder could not believe his luck, that he did not have to fight to pass through Hyena Land. Why had he not done this before? Yet, the skulls reminded him that others did not make it.

Kinder followed a winding river that could not be crossed except where the river's flow was broken by great rocks. On the other side, the rocky land offered good places for hiding in case of need.

He suddenly saw a small hunting group ahead of him, that had already spied him. They were wary and had two wolves with them. *Who was this lone person with a bear?* they must have wondered. Maybe they thought he was a *Fierce One*....

Kinder came closer and asked for a woman named Huntress. "She is my lost sister."

One answered, saying he knew of no woman who hunted. The group debated among themselves.

"He has a bear. Is he not a *Fierce One*?"

"A bear is fierce, is it not? We must kill him."

"No Fierce Ones tame animals. As for a fighting man and a bear, it's best to let them pass."

The bear saved Kinder's journey in this way, for the Wolf People did not often allow lone strangers to roam their land.

"How do I quickly pass through your land?" asked Kinder before taking his leave.

The Wolf People advised, "Stay close to this side of the river. Do not cross to the other side, for the Land of Snakes lies there."

Kinder thanked them and moved on, sensing that his chances of finding Huntress were small. He did not know where to look. He sensed, too, an air of danger. The Wolf People had spoken as if Fierce Ones were wandering about.

On the following day, he came upon three of them, who smelled and had bones hanging from their belts. The Fierce Ones had stopped and were staring at him, a darkness about their faces.

Kinder stood still, crossed his arms, and stared back at them. The bear watched too and made a low growl.

The Fierce Ones moved on. A Fierce One was worth two *New Ones*, but a bear was worth two Fierce Ones. The odds were too close, and they did not attack. Even if things had gone well for them, a bear could badly wound or kill one. And being wounded badly was as bad as death. The Fierce Ones did not fear wounds or death, but today they chose neither.

Danger passed and Kinder considered. The Fierce Ones would attack the Wolf People here. He must find Huntress before that happens and take her home.

Two days later, he chanced upon another small group. They had no wolves, and they wanted an animal with them, even if it was a bear.

Kinder refused. The group had heard of a woman who hunted further downriver. Kinder pressed on, traveling by night.

When Kinder woke, the light was painful, and he felt a throbbing pain from his head. He could not get up, for his hands and legs were bound. *What had happened? How was it possible?* Straining, he pulled up his head to look. Three Fierce Ones were eating.

Then Kinder realized his bear had died, and they were feasting on her. A Fierce One, gnawing on a bone, noticed him and laughed.

CHAPTER VII

Fierce Ones

At first they did not seem so fierce. They unbound him and let him get up if he wanted to stretch. Kinder stood up and looked around, careful to not make any sudden movements. They seemed to have no concern that he might run away. They were trackers, and his stick was shattered. How could they have crept up on him? It was because he had been so tired, and not careful enough in choosing the place he slept.

Why were they keeping him alive? Were they waiting to kill him because they had bear food now? Dead flesh did not keep. Or were they possibly wanting him to join them? Four would be stronger. Maybe they did not want to kill someone who had the power to tame a bear. Kinder felt stricken for his bear's death, but he had no time to grieve.

The group hardly noticed him. Kinder could not understand their talk, which was more like gestures and grunting sounds. He sensed they would kill him on a whim. He would have to wait for a chance to run and make good his escape. If they caught him again, they would surely kill him. Kinder resolved to study them, like he had studied the way of bears.

Kinder knew he would need to do more than wait for the right time to escape, that he needed to come up with a plan. He decided to play the part of a bear, to move in a bear way and make bear noises.

At first, the Fierce Ones looked on with puzzlement, then they laughed. It made sense. He had been with a bear and spent much time alone with a bear. When the Fierce Ones traveled, they signaled for him to follow.

The Fierce Ones went swiftly along the river, stopping only to examine the tracks of people fleeing before them. Kinder growled, grunted, and ate leaves. It didn't bother the Fierce Ones as long as he kept up.

Kinder knew he had only so much time before they would kill him. Along the way, Kinder caught a large rabbit for them. The Fierce Ones laughed and ate it without offering him any.

The next morning Kinder saw something he had not seen before. A Fierce One killed a young female lion. One had sprung in his path and he killed her with his bare hands.

Kinder saw their strength. No wonder they did not worry about him. One alone could kill a lion without a sharp stick.

Kinder was not offered any lion meat. He showed that it didn't matter to him, and he dug about for roots and grubs. He would pose no threat to them.

The next couple of days food became less, and the Fierce Ones started eyeing Kinder. Tonight, he must try to escape, he realized. It would be a dangerous time, for night predators would be about.

The Fierce Ones kept a night look out, who didn't often look Kinder's way. The lookout smelled him, however. When Kinder went off a piece to relieve himself, the Fierce One would stand nearby.

Kinder came up with a plan to leave his skin behind and stuff them with leaves. This would leave his smell and shape.

Kinder fled naked into the night, and had not gone far before he heard the howls of Fierce Ones. Kinder ran. He had speed, but he was in a land he did not know. He had to go fast, but not too fast, lest he injure himself. When he next heard the howls, they sounded nearer.

Kinder's plan went only so far, for he was in a strange land. He thought of climbing trees, a high one that would just support his slender weight. But the Fierce Ones might bend the tree itself.

Their howls were nearing, and Kinder tried to quell his feelings of fear. Panicked prey was easier to catch.

Then Kinder remembered the danger the Wolf People had described on the other side of the river. If he crossed it, the Fierce Ones might not follow.

The first twilight was coming, when Kinder reached a widening river with a rocky way across. On the other side, dark angular rocks filled the bank. It held unknown dangers, but he had no choice.

Kinder crossed the river, using touch as much as sight. More than once he was pressed against rocks and could barely free himself. Kinder reached the far side, then collapsed in exhaustion. In plain sight on a gravelly ground, he considered calling upon the Elements to somehow help him. Summoning his own strength, he crawled toward the rocks and had almost reached them when he heard shouting from the far shore. The Fierce Ones had spotted him. They paused only a short time before stepping into the river.

Kinder got up and staggered toward the rocks. He would not get far before they would catch up to him. What should he do? Find a high place to fight, or an opening in the ground to hide with the snakes? He looked about for holes, but they were too shallow or their entrance too narrow.

Kinder went deeper into the rocky country. The howls of the Fierce Ones reached a new pitch, and he knew they had reached shore. He saw a diamond patterned snake and felt himself shake.

Sooner than expected, Kinder found an opening that had some depth. Here he would make his stand. He might kill one, maybe two Fierce Ones. If he could convince them that he could do them some harm, he might survive, for the Fierce Ones calculated their odds.

When howls blasted into his opening, Kinder tried to refrain from shaking. He must cry out to show he was strong. Had he not been named Howler? But Kinder lost his voice. He did not feel his name, only weakness and exhaustion. Images flashed through his head:

Huntress who did not fear to hunt, and Gazelle, who had let him go with tears. They would never see him again.

The Fierce Ones wondered at this silent prey. Was it weakness or strength?

Kinder then remembered Bough. Had she not faced a lion? She was both hunter and mother, and the one who named him Howler. Kinder summoned the roar of a bear, and the sound was fierce, echoing off the chamber's walls.

The Fierce Ones stared into the darkness. *Had the man changed into a bear? If he was a bear, would he not kill at least one of them?*

Kinder listened; the Fierce Ones were not leaving. They had come too far to not take their prey, even if one of them were to die.

CHAPTER VIII

Kinder Fights

Kinder prepared to fight and die. And as he searched for a loose stone, he felt something brush his leg. It was a giant snake. Kinder did not move, and the snake continued on. It had been disturbed by his roar. Slowly, it wove its way outside the cave.

The Fierce Ones killed and ate the snake. Their hunger left them and they left too.

The snake had saved him, but Kinder was alone and naked in a rocky land filled with snakes. He waited, listening to the silence for a long while before venturing out. The Fierce Ones had left only the head of the snake behind, and Kinder did not eat it. He would follow the river and find Huntress.

The river bank became filled with briers, making for a tough passage. Kinder saw the brambles as safety. He went through them, streaking his body with red, and dipped in the river when they became too thick.

The brambles ended. In the river small islands appeared, filled with birds and food, and out of his reach.

When Kinder came upon a small group of Wolf People, he looked like a wild man, even a *Fierce One*. That he had no skins, or a stick made him appear even more dangerous. Kinder asked if they had a skin, and if they knew a woman named Huntress. They fearfully threw him half of a skin and went on.

A second group was larger and did not answer him. They considered killing him. But Kinder made signs as if he were a *Fierce One*, and they stepped away.

When Kinder reached a third group of Wolf People, who were encamped, their leader spoke back. "What bloodied man comes to us, asking about a woman who hunts? Maybe you would be happier with some food."

Kinder stood silent and determined. Had he finally found Huntress?

Flint saw his look. "If you have a claim, what do you offer, man with a half skin?"

Kinder's heart raced; she might be here. He had nothing to offer, no plan beyond finding her. He could only think to say, "I will fight for her."

Flint laughed. "Why should we risk a man dying? Shouldn't we just throw rocks at you and shoo you away?"

"Ask the woman, for she knows me. Huntress will go with me, when she knows who I am."

"Do you think that she alone decides her fate? But she has spoken of a man.... When she returns from hunting, I will ask."

Kinder waited a distance away.

When Huntress returned, the men kept her from rushing to Kinder.

Flint warned, "Maybe this man has changed. He looks like a half *Fierce One*."

Huntress answered, "He is my brother."

"He does not look to be your brother. You would go with this Wild Man?"

"I will."

Flint did not think it wise. "You have become one of us. But he says he will fight for you. We will give him that chance. Do you accept this?"

Huntress paused. "To have someone become hurt or die for me is not necessary."

"We will not set a person against him, but a wolf," Flint answered.

Huntress cried out in alarm, "Who can survive a wolf?"

"It is my decision. It will be an older wolf. One or the other must die, for that is the way of the Wolf People. It is better for him to fight the wolf than one of us."

Huntress looked toward Kinder, who remained determined. She realized he would not accept her refusal and would fight anyway.

"I accept," she said, lowering her head.

Kinder considered. It did not seem possible to win, even if it were an old wolf. And he would not have the benefit of surprise. But could he come all this way for Huntress and leave without her?

He stepped toward the group, accepting the offer, then was surprised when a male spoke. "I will fight him."

All looked in the voice's direction. It was Sharpener.

Huntress cried, "No!" for she had grown to love the man. She could not bear to see this either.

Flint hesitated. "You will fight this young man?"

"Was this woman not given to me? Can I not fight for her a second time? She is not the wolf's to give away."

The man's words were true. Still Flint asked, "You would go against this woman's wish, a woman you defended?"

"Is this not the way of the Wolf People?" guessed Sharpener. Flint did not understand this man, yet it was so.

"Give the old man his stick. We have not much time, for Fierce Ones are about."

Kinder tried to size up his opponent and wondered at the confusion. Why would this older man want to fight him? Why would he say he was acting for Huntress? People had strange ways, and Kinder let go of his confusion. It did not matter why. He had to kill this man.

The older man looked experienced, and his stick was long and sharp. Kinder steeled himself. If the man had done much fighting, this could be hard. But it was better odds than facing a wolf.

Kinder sparred to test his opponent, to sense his strengths and weaknesses. The man was strong, nearly as strong as a young man. He was quick enough, too. *This would not be an easy kill,* thought Kinder. *But it will have to be done.* The man did not have the look of someone with battle hate, and Kinder wondered if he could just knock him out. That would not be as easy; sometimes it was just easier to kill.

Kinder furiously pressed the man to further test him. One of his blows penetrated the man's defenses and glanced his leg. But Kinder went too far and was off balance for a moment. The man could have struck him, but did not. No one else had noticed, for it happened so fast.

Kinder looked at the man, wondering. His face gave no hint.

Once when they grappled, Kinder asked under his breath, "Why do you not fully fight me?"

"You must kill me," answered the man.

Confusion swept over Kinder. "I do not want to kill you."

"You must, if you want the woman to go with you."

The old man kept fighting. Some blows grazed Kinder and left blood. It was like the man was trying to strike air. Once the old man left himself exposed, but Kinder pulled back his thrust, leaving only a shallow wound.

It seemed to enrage the man that he wasn't wounded enough. Kinder pressed on, but his confusion grew. He could not think of a stranger battle. Could it be? When Kinder left an opening, the man held back.

Kinder wondered. *Maybe he is a Power come to test me.* "Who are you?" he asked under his breath.

The man offered only his gaze, as if to say there would be no answers until one of them died. Kinder must kill, but he could not. He could not bring himself to kill someone who would not fully defend himself.

The Wolf People thought it was a good fight, and they waited for the death blow.

Kinder was angry, but he could not put his anger into this fight. The man, who would not kill him, had a power he could not place.

Something in Kinder changed, and he tossed his stick down. "I will not fight," he declared, his actions surprising even himself. "The old man can do as he wants." Kinder stood motionless.

Huntress cried out, "No!"

The Wolf People looked to Sharpener to finish the kill.

Sharpener tossed his stick down too. "Who can kill a man who chooses not to fight? Among my people, the fight he has given is good enough. I offer him the woman who was given me."

Flint was perplexed and did not know what to do. Something had happened that he could not explain. The old man had fought and won, yet acted as if he had lost by offering her.

"It is the rule that one dies," Flint countered.

The Wolf People murmured their affirmation, and some even raised their sticks.

Then the Silent One spoke. "It is also the rule that one who throws down his stick can be given mercy. Yet both have thrown down theirs. So it is up to you, Flint, to decide, and can you not grant mercy to both?"

At this point Huntress broke free, came to Kinder, and wrapped her arms around him. "If my brother dies, I will die too!"

What could Flint do? He was a hard man, but he was not cruel. And, as the Silent One had said, he could grant mercy. Still, it was an unusual to do so for both.

"The Sharpener may give her away," Flint finally said.

Kinder and Huntress embraced, but their happiness was short lived. A wolf man among them did not think Flint's decision was right.

He turned on Sharpener and wounded him deeply in the stomach. The wolf man's face looked as if he were part *Fierce One*.

CHAPTER IX

Island of No Cares

Kinder raised his stick to protect the old man from being wounded further. But the surrounding hunters had raised their sticks, too.

"No more! I have decided," Flint ordered.

Huntress tended to Sharpener. Kinder, too, was by him.

The old man was gasping. He grasped Kinder's hand and spoke fast. "I knew the Trembling One. She had a boy. She–"

Sharpener went unconscious.

The half *Fierce One* was not settled. He continued raising questions about their woman being taken away.

"I have decided," Flint repeated, raising his staff.

The half *Fierce One* was not ready to fight Flint, so he backed down. But Kinder saw his look was unchanged and that he would one day challenge Flint.

"We must leave now," said Kinder.

So the Wolf People allowed Huntress to leave, and she took Giving Flower as well.

"Who is this?" asked Kinder.

"It is a child I have claimed as my own."

Kinder sized her up. "Is she not safer with the Wolf People?"

"In time, they will kill her."

"Let her come then. We must go before the Half-one tries to kill us all."

Huntress took a last look at Sharpener, whose face had calmed. She wondered if he would survive, but it was likely she would never know.

Kinder looked to Huntress's face and saw her grief, and he too felt sadness. *Who was this man he fought?* he wondered. *How did he know my mother?*

Hurriedly, the three left downriver.

Kinder was happy and anxious. He had finally found Huntress, but now he had to defend two more in perilous lands. Huntress could hunt, but Giving Flower did not look as if she could help with much. It seemed she could hardly speak. At best, it was as if he and Huntress had gained a child together.

After they left the Wolf People, Kinder showed his anger. "Why did you choose this one? She increases our danger––making noises, stopping to look at flowers, and falling down."

They argued like they used to, and Kinder didn't know what to think. Had nothing changed?

Huntress defended her. "She is harmless, a Giver of Flowers. Why should she die? Do you not have the name Kinder now?"

She spoke rightly of the way of *New Ones*. But *New Ones* or not, they had to survive. What would they do if they ran into Fierce Ones? The newly made family rested, and Kinder wondered how they would make their way.

"You finally came for me," said Huntress, coming to his side.

Kinder was still irritated. "Didn't I promise I would?"

"You did, but you did not have to come."

"We are like brother and sister. Did not Bough tell us to look out for each other?"

Huntress summoned her courage and looked Kinder in the eye. It seemed harder than facing an animal in the wild. "Is there not something more? I am a woman; you are a man."

Kinder turned his head away.

"We argue and fight," he said, digging his stick into the earth.

"I do not care." She tried to take his hand.

"We must go on," said Kinder, pulling free. "We have to find a safe place. There are Fierce Ones about."

Huntress wondered if her mother had been wrong. *Is Kinder just a brother to me?*

Kinder's fears proved true. The sun was high when they almost ran into five Fierce Ones resting by the river. Huntress held her hand over Giving Flower's mouth. They were close, but carefully backed away, moving downriver until they heard the Fierce One's rough sounds no more. Kinder knew that if their scent was found, they would surely be followed. They must get as far away as possible.

They followed the thick growth as they moved downriver. With Giving Flower, they blazed a path, however. There were no rocks or places to shelter for the night. The Fierce Ones would surely find them if they came looking. How could they travel through the night in the brush with a child?

They went to the river to drink and found it had widened and held islands. One island was not so far from shore. Kinder decided their best hope was to go to that island, to rest in safety and wait until danger passed.

The water was fast. There was a time in the month when it was lower, but it was only half way to that time. Kinder guessed they could cross, but not with Giving Flower.

Kinder and Huntress argued again. "We must leave her behind," he told Huntress, but she refused. Kinder could not believe her. "You would choose this Small One over us?"

Tears came to Huntress's eyes. "How can I give up our child!"

She had said *our*, but it was not his child, and one who was less than a halfling. But Kinder saw, in Huntress, the mother who had defended them when they were young.

How would they make their way with this child? he wondered. *It would only take one slip in crossing the river. One time for her to cry out, so that the Fierce Ones heard.*

What could Kinder do? He realized that he would have to do as Huntress wished.

"Maybe there is a way," he said at last. "We can hold hands, and I will carry her where the current runs deepest."

Giving Flower did not seem to know the danger. If Huntress went, she went too.

From rock to rock, they made their way. At one point Huntress and Giving Flower were afraid to move. "You can make it!" called Kinder, his hands tensing.

Kinder pulled them to the last group of rocks, a few feet from the island. The last part was deep and swift.

Kinder picked up Giving Flower and swung her behind his back. He stepped carefully as the current pulled at him, leaving him unsteady. He took a second step, with Huntress close behind. With his third step, Kinder lost his footing, and he and Giving Flower tumbled.

The river swept them into a pocket of a nearby rock. The water pressed at them, tearing at their skins.

Kinder saw Huntress's panicked face, her body pinned, unable to move. Giving Flower's head was under water, her hair streaming above. Kinder barely had the strength to move sideways against the current. He reached Giving Flower, lifted her head, and she gasped, laughing wildly. Did she not fear death?

The water was like a great weight, pinning them only a few feet from the island. Closer to the island, the current was faster.

Exhausted, Kinder said, "When the water lessens, we will move."

"When will the water lessen?" asked Huntress.

Kinder did not answer. He did not know when, only that it would be some time.

"Can you not command the river?" asked Huntress.

Kinder had almost forgotten that he was a *Child of the Elements*. But he had only thought of the sky, clouds, and rain as the Elements, not the river.

The river felt so powerful, and he felt so weak. It was impossible, but he would try. Kinder raised his hands and cried, "River, turn your power away!"

The sun slowly set. Nothing happened. The rushing water got colder, and they started shivering. Bough had joined them on the rock, Kinder catching her. She inched to Giving Flower and held her.

"The river is taking away our life!" cried Huntress. "If the river does not obey you, we must leave it or we will die."

Kinder knew it was so. He knew he could make it alone, but he could not leave the others behind. They were only becoming more tired from the river pressing into them. They must do something.

"I will carry you across," he told Huntress.

"Take Giving Flower first."

Kinder thought it impossible. "How can I come back twice? The river is like a Fierce One!"

"You must."

Kinder's anger flared, and he slapped her. "Why preserve her life above yours! You are my sister!"

Huntress let go of a deep cry of pain—not from the blow, which was not hard—but because the one she loved had hit her.

"You will find a way," cried Huntress through her tears. "You are a *Child of the Elements!* You can defeat the river."

Kinder felt ashamed. "I will take her first."

He grabbed hold of the Small One. Although her face showed no fear, she clung for her life.

She was light, but Kinder's steps were unsteady. One time a pain came to his foot, and red swam through the water.

Kinder howled at the river. He should let go of Giving Flower and come back for his sister. But Huntress called out. "You are almost there! The river is letting you pass!"

Ignoring the pain, Kinder tore through the water. Somehow he made it and they collapsed on the island.

They had made it, but Kinder wailed. He did not have the strength to bring Huntress back. Even if he was able to make it to her, how would he carry her? As light as Giving Flower was, he had just made it. There was his wound too, and the blood had flowed in the water and taken his strength. All he could see was that they would both be lost to the river, and Giving Flower would be left alone to starve on the island.

Huntress saw his look. "Care for Giving Flower," she wailed, but still in the wail was a plea for him to come.

Kinder knew he must think of a way. Night was falling and Huntress would be left to die of cold or be swept away. What could he do? He thought of Bough. She had always known what to do. He remembered what she had told him. "Look for a new way. We are *New Ones.*"

Yes, he remembered, she had saved him once when he had fallen in the water. She had used a stick.

Kinder searched the island and found a large fallen bough. He dragged it, his foot leaving blood prints. He lifted it high and let it fall in the water ahead of Huntress. It landed against a rock next to her.

Kinder held one end down with his body and called to Huntress. Somehow she must have the strength to pull herself along the branch.

Huntress crossed, came out cold and blue.

Kinder rubbed her body, then laid next to her. He held her for a long time. After the cold and shivering, she became hot and still. Huntress lived, and when morning came, they still held each other.

That day, Kinder was the weaker for his lost blood. Huntress became Healer, washed his wound, and bound it with plants.

It took days for their strength to fully return. But they came to have many happy days on the island. Giving Flower was fun to watch, and she seemed happy no matter what happened. The birds had no fear of people, and they were easy to catch. Fish abounded in shallow places and could be caught by hand. They had no animals from which to make new skins, for their old ones were torn. So Healer made garments of grass and feathers.

"It is a new thing," said Healer, laughing. "This is the Island of No Cares."

Since the time of passing over the waters, Huntress and Kinder had slept in one another's arms. Giving Flower would sleep by them sometimes, but she also found a little hollow near them.

Kinder learned the ways of women. One day he saw blood coming from Huntress. He thought she was wounded, that something must have bitten her. Huntress laughed. "It is a wound that comes to a grown woman every moon. No animal did this."

Huntress taught him another new thing: how to throw a stick. "How did you learn to do this?" he asked.

"One of the Powers showed me in a dream."

"Will this Power fight for you?" asked Kinder.

"The Power helps my aim to be true."

"Are you a *Woman of Power*?"

"You already know my power," Huntress answered.

THE SEASON WAS CHANGING, and Kinder wondered if the Fierce Ones had left the land. There had been no sign of them, and they kept to the far side of the island where they would not be in view. Something, however, happened that meant they must journey soon. Huntress had signs of a child. If she grew too large, how could she travel?

Kinder decided to leave, but they had waited too long. The next day they heard Fierce Ones moving along the shore, and Giving Flower was nowhere in sight.

They found her standing on the wrong side of the island in plain view.

The Fierce Ones saw her and howled.

CHAPTER X

Raging River

There were eight of them—the largest group of Fierce Ones Kinder had seen. At first, he thought they were safe. Crossing the river would be too difficult and dangerous for them. Standing on rocks by the island's shore, a man with a stick could possibly hold them off.

The Fierce Ones were looking their way, calculating the odds.

Kinder stood up with Huntress, with sticks in hand, letting the Fierce Ones know they were willing to fight.

They were eight though. What could Kinder and Huntress do?

The Fierce Ones stayed, thinking they had easy prey if they could but reach the island. They set up camp, knowing they could take their time. Maybe they would wait for the river to lower itself....

Kinder and Huntress stayed awake in shifts, with Kinder taking the night. They took turns sharpening more spears. There was only so much straight wood lying about, and spears were hard to make.

Giving Flower was not aware of the danger. She threw stones toward the Fierce Ones, but at other times she threw flowers.

Kinder did not bother to rebuke her.

The Fierce Ones were waiting to see if the river would fall. The next day, they became impatient and tested the water. One came halfway across, up to a deep point. Kinder had a stick ready, but the man was only looking. Kinder thought of throwing his spear, but he decided to wait until one came closer and in rushing water.

The Fierce One rejoined his group and readied them.

"They are too many," said Huntress. "How will we stop them if they all come?"

"We have five sticks now, and we have rocks."

Huntress looked Kinder in the eye and spoke a hard thing. "Do not let us be taken alive. Promise to kill me first. Then Giving Flower."

"How can I kill who I love, and our child?" asked Kinder.

Huntress lowered her face and did not wipe away her tears. He had spoken of his love and of their child.

Half-trembling, Huntress said, "They have captured me before. You must promise."

Kinder promised, then said, "We are two strong, and we have the river on our side. We can defeat the Fierce Ones!"

"I have fought a Wolf Man, but the child within slows me. I can throw a stick, but I cannot hold the stick and fight a Fierce One."

Kinder held back his tears. She had already fought a man and lived.

"It is wise for you to fight at a distance, Kinder agreed.

The Fierce Ones did not come all at once, but three set out in the middle of the day when the river was lower. They reached a long rock and paused.

It happened quickly, the three churning in the river towards them. They were only steps away when Kinder and Huntress threw their spears. Kinder hit the first man square in the chest, and he tumbled downriver. Huntress's spear cut through the water and pierced the second man in the leg. The Fierce One howled and, with the help of the third, went back to the long rock.

Three spears and six whole men left, thought Kinder. He brought out two more spears, like there were many more.

The Fierce Ones retreated to the shore and glared at them. They did their calculation. Maybe the price would be seen as too high, and they would leave. But having lost one, they stayed, wanting revenge.

Night descended. "There is something more you can do," said Huntress. "You must call on the river to rise."

In the night Kinder called on the river. "I feel nothing," he said afterwards.

Huntress was silent. She gave a small, sharp stick to Kinder that she had placed under her belt.

"You will not need it?" asked Kinder, not knowing how he could defeat them. "And when they come, what will we do with Giving Flower? She wanders about still."

"I will place her on the high rock, which juts over the river on the far side. She does not know how to climb down. We will go there if all else fails."

Kinder saw that was wise. From there, they might hold off the Fierce Ones, or jump to their death on rocks that jutted from the river below.

Neither Kinder nor Huntress could sleep. Kinder said, "We have killed."

"It is not the first time," said Huntress.

Kinder looked at Huntress and wondered. "Yes, we have killed animals, but not ones who are half men and half animals."

Huntress felt the Healer in her. "It hurts, even though they are Fierce Ones."

Huntress's expression suddenly changed, and she felt her belly. "The baby in me moves."

The next day the Fierce Ones sent five men, leaving the wounded man behind with another.

In the night Kinder had made another stick, although it was only half-sharpened.

Giving Flower did not like being left alone on a rock where she could not wander. She wailed. She did not understand and thought they were leaving her. Clinging to Huntress, she had spoken the word, "Mother."

Huntress was amazed, for she had not heard her say the full word before. Huntress tried to soothe her, but Giving Flower sobbed and wailed.

In the morning Kinder looked up at the clouds and realized that he had no plan but Huntress's. But this plan was too late in working. Still, he opened his arms again and summoned the rain. The clouds moved in the sky, but there was no darkness or feeling of rain in them.

This time the Fierce Ones would not rely on their strength alone, and they brought stones. The Fierce Ones planned to hurl rocks and keep the *New Ones* away so they couldn't hurl their throwing sticks.

Kinder saw their odds of success diminish. Still, he studied the men and saw that there seemed to be a half New One among them. It was in his eyes and the way he gestured.

There was no plan against so many, Kinder knew. *Could I really kill Huntress?*

The five men reached the long rock. Then three began to cross the last part, while two remained and hurled rocks.

Kinder and Huntress stepped back, dodging rocks. The first man was almost there. Kinder dashed forward, threw his spear, and missed. Huntress followed with her throw and hit him in the side. The Fierce One toppled into the river with a wail, but the second and third had not stopped.

Kinder used his last sharpened spear. A kill was worth a spear. He threw it true, hitting the second man in the belly. The Fierce One, big and strong, wavered, then fell in the water. The third man went back to the long rock and urged the other two. Soon three Fierce Ones were crossing, and Kinder had only one blunt spear.

He held onto the spear. Huntress threw rocks, but the men brushed them away.

Kinder looked at Huntress. They had failed. Three Fierce Ones were almost upon them.

He waited for the first man to come close to shore. If they could topple one, it might topple the line. The first Fierce One was only two steps away when Kinder crashed his stick down on the man's shoulder. But the Fierce One grabbed the stick and wrenched it from Kinder's hands.

Huntress threw a rock that hit the man, but he shrugged off the blow.

Three came on the island's shore. Still, Huntress had some luck. The last man was smaller and lost his grip on the one ahead of him. Huntress threw a stone and hit the unsteady one in the head. The wounded Fierce One retreated, going back to the long rock.

It started raining. The river would rise, but it was too late. Two Fierce Ones had stepped ashore, and Kinder and Huntress had only one blunt stick. They fled.

Huntress and Kinder went to the high rock and joined Giving Flower, afraid and sobbing.

Below, the Fierce Ones were rustling in the brush just beyond. Soon they would find the jutting rock.

"Do it now!" she cried.

The rain was pouring, and the wind had picked up.

"I can't. I feel power coming. We can kill the Fierce Ones!"

"How can you kill with rain and a short stick? Kill us now! You have promised!"

"I cannot kill those whom I love!"

It was not good to break a promise, but Kinder saw there was something greater than this promise.

"If you cannot, I will," she said, pulling a sharp rock from a crevice.

"Wait, I have a plan," said Kinder, and he turned. He had no plan that would kill two. Maybe he could kill one, but what plan could kill two?

The rain delayed the Fierce Ones, and they used sticks to poke about in the brush. They laughed, for they felt no threat.

Kinder would have to surprise them. He came down the rock and found a slit between two boulders, large enough for only one to pass. It did not work. The man went around him, then toward the high rock. Kinder had to reveal himself. He threw a stone, and the Fierce One howled, signaling his companion.

The other one came running, near where Kinder hid. It was the Half-one, smarter but not as strong. Kinder would have surprise, and he would have to win fast. He tripped the Half-one and grappled him.

When they hit the ground, Kinder's ribs flashed with pain, but the Fierce One hit his head against a rock. He was stunned for several moments.

Kinder grabbed his stick and struck the man on the back. Then he felt a searing pain in his right shoulder and dropped his stick. The second Fierce One had pierced him. Kinder knew to move quickly, but not which way. He moved left and the blow just missed. He lowered himself, as if buckling from pain, grabbed dirt, and threw it up in the man-animal's face. Then Kinder fled, wounded.

His legs were good, but one arm was not. He found Huntress with Giving Flower. She saw his blood, his wounded arm. Huntress started shaking and sunk down, her hands placed on her swollen belly. Kinder held her and saw the stone in her hand. He grabbed the stone from her and threw it into the river.

"No!" she screamed.

Kinder looked down and saw two Fierce Ones climbing. They did not seem to be slowed at all. Hope was gone, yet he heard a distant roll of thunder.

The rain had become stronger, the river higher. Kinder held out his arms and howled. That was all he could think to do. He had only the short, sharp stick left, and it was needed to kill themselves.

Lightning struck nearby. The Fierce Ones paused, then roared as they spied them on top of the rock.

"If you can't kill me, at least kill Giving Flower," cried Huntress.

"Stand up," ordered Kinder. Huntress stood up, grasping Giving Flower in front of her.

The two Fierce men were halfway up the stone.

Kinder raised his hand to strike Giving Flower.

The rain was coming in sheets; he looked at the swollen water passing in a torrent, covering the rocks. He pulled his hand away and yelled, "Jump! Jump into the river!"

Giving Flower tried to pull away. Huntress knew that jumping was likely death, but they would die together. She held tightly onto Giving Flower.

A Fierce One's hand had appeared over the rock ledge. Kinder reached out with his left hand and stabbed the hand. The Fierce One howled. The Half-one leapt up and was standing before them.

Then Kinder clutched Giving Flower from Huntress and jumped, and Huntress followed them into the raging river.

CHAPTER XI

Gathering

The deep water raged fast and hurled them downriver. They glanced over rocks and swept past whirlpools. They were torn from each other. Kinder and Huntress could swim, but Giving Flower had never learned. Huntress called out, "Don't fight the water, go with the river!"

The next thing Kinder knew were voices.

"Be careful. Don't touch them."

"The two are wounded—fresh blood."

"Should we let them die or kill them?"

"Do not help them. They may be half Fierce Ones."

Kinder could not move or open his eyes. The voices had said there were two. Was it Huntress or Giving Flower?

There was silence, and Kinder forgot how badly his body hurt.

A female voice said, "The woman is with child. We could take her with us."

Kinder coughed, half gasped. Huntress had lived, and the voices were deciding their fate. He was too weak to speak and knew the danger. He smelled a wolf's scent and realized they must be Wolf People. Kinder's eyes opened a little, but he had not the strength to speak.

If they were left by the Wolf People, they would not survive. Huntress was wounded too—how badly?

Kinder wanted to cry out, but he could not.

"Look at his wounds; he is a warrior," said a strong voice. "The woman, too, is scarred. Are these not marks of Fierce Ones?"

"Perhaps they fought the Fierce Ones," a woman considered.

"It is safest to kill," said the strong voice. "Too many of us have died."

Kinder tried to say a word, to call out "Huntress!" A moan escaped him.

"See, he cannot speak," said the man, and he readied his stick.

"You would kill her too?" asked the Wolf Woman. "She is not large enough to be a Fierce One." The woman had already let go of Kinder's life.

"If this man is a Fierce One, the woman must share in his ways," reasoned the strong voice.

Kinder tried to raise his arm, but only his fingers moved. Then he heard confusion and voices shouting, "Look! Over there!"

There was an agonizing silence, waiting. Something was happening.... Kinder lifted his head and saw a blur.

Then he heard sobbing and the word, "Mother."

"Look!" exclaimed the woman. "They are not Fierce Ones, for this Small One has spoken."

Giving Flower had survived.

"It is a word and from a simple child," protested the strong voice.

"What Fierce One truly speaks?" asked the woman. "They wail, howl, and cry, but they do not speak words. And if they did, would it be Mother?"

"It must be so," said another man's voice. "This child cannot be a Fierce One, and the woman she calls Mother cannot be one either."

An older woman's voice spoke among them. "They are not Fierce Ones; they are not Wolf People ... The man and woman must be *New Ones*. I know their ways. They do not kill Simple Ones."

The Strong Voice doubted if the wounded man and women were New Ones.

"Can you not see it?" the older woman asked. "He must be the warrior who killed the three Fierce Ones we saw wash downriver. He must be a great fighter. The woman helped him. Do you not see her scars?"

"We have need of fighters who can kill Fierce Ones," said the Strong Voice. "We will carry them."

Another voice protested, "It will slow us down. What if the Fierce Ones come upon us? How will we flee?"

"We will keep the warrior, his woman, and the Simple One," said the Strong Voice. "It is decided," said more voices one by one.

Kinder smiled as he was raised up. Giving Flower had saved them by speaking a word.

The three were carried till late in the day, then set down. The Wolf People had reached their safe place and rested. Kinder's and Huntress's bodies were sore all over. Kinder's bones were whole and his wound was healing in his arm. But he could not rise and had only the strength to say a few words. Huntress had broken an arm, and her legs were unsteady when she rose. Giving Flower did not seem to be hurt, except for bruises on her legs and arms, and a cut on her forehead. The Wolf People took care of them, and the child within Huntress grew. Their leader was named Breaker, and the woman who had spoken on their behalf was called Rain.

When Huntress answered their questions, the Wolf People were amazed to hear how they had fought and killed Fierce Ones. Huntress told how brave Kinder was and how he led them. She admitted, when she was asked, that she had killed a Fierce One, even though it was two.

One day, Kinder woke with Healer's hands upon him. He had gained his voice back and had the strength to rise.

The Wolf People were in awe of Kinder and Huntress, the ones who had killed Fierce Ones. They had fought them off before, but had not killed any.

Kinder was not used to being respected among men, in having bigger men defer to him or have women look at him in a special way.

The Wolf People showed nearly the same respect to Huntress. She had fought and killed too. She was under Kinder's protection and with child, so no man bothered her.

Even Giving Flower was given respect. She was there when they fought the Fierce Ones, even if she had not helped. One of the younger Wolf Men seemed to favor her. He stuttered in his speech and was short, but he seemed strong and true. He did small things for her, such as giving her a gift of a stone which sparkled. Huntress and Kinder smiled, for there seemed to be a future for them here.

In the days that followed, they heard disturbing news from Breaker. Things were happening since they had been on the Island of No Cares. The land by the river was being overrun by Fierce Ones. The Wolf People were considering going to another land, to the Drylands, Snake Land, or even Hyena Land. Anywhere might be safer, and maybe they could go beyond and find a new land. Some thought they must stay and fight. There were other Wolf People with wolves who could kill Fierce Ones. Maybe if the groups gathered together, they could survive. There was talk of summoning others.

Kinder's strength returned, and Huntress could walk. Her arm still hurt, and she would not be able to hurl sticks for some time.

One day, two Wolf People came among them from another group.

"It is time to leave," Breaker announced after speaking to them. "A full moon is coming, and a gathering is happening on the hill where the Old Ones are buried. A man there summons the Wolf Peoples and says we must fight. Fierce Ones are roaming in large groups, killing all they come across. A half New One leads them. Time is short. We must leave in the morning."

"My woman is full and will bear a child soon," said Kinder. "Should I not stay with her?"

"We need you," Breaker replied. "She is still strong enough to come with us, and she is safer with the group."

Huntress got up; she was willing to go. She was smiling, for Kinder had said before "my woman."

Kinder realized that Breaker was not ordering him and letting him decide. Even the leader, who was stronger than Kinder, was granting him great respect. Yet Kinder saw in this man's eyes that he placed much hope in him. All the others remained silent, waiting for his answer.

"You are a New One and a warrior. You can help us defeat the Fierce Ones," Breaker declared, holding out a stick.

Kinder took the stick and the Wolf People howled.

The group traveled and more bands joined them. Some men came and went, seeking out others. The Wolf Peoples had nine wolves in all. That was their best hope, for a wolf was an even match for a Fierce One.

Breaker walked by Kinder's side. Kinder saw his hope and spoke. "I am not a great warrior. Huntress knows how to throw sticks and wound. There was rain too, and we had luck."

Breaker was not deterred. "I know *New Ones* do not like to speak of their great deeds."

"Only the *Powers* do great deeds," Kinder returned.

"I have heard from your woman that you call on the storm and rain," countered Breaker. "However things happened, you defeated many Fierce Ones. By now, all the Wolf People have heard about you. You must lead us against the Fierce Ones."

Kinder thought this crazy. He was not of great size, nor had he fought much. He had some luck and help from the Elements.

"Who is the one who summons?" Kinder asked.

"He is not young, but he has killed Fierce Ones. The Summoner says you are the one who will lead us."

Kinder wondered how this could be so, and he turned to look at Huntress. *She is a warrior too and not given half the credit. She has not given up fighting, even though she is hurt and with child.*

Huntress looked into his eyes; she had hope in him too.

"I will lead," decided Kinder.

CHAPTER XII

Lion's Mouth

As the group journeyed, their numbers increased. Word had spread: "The New One, who has killed many Fierce Ones, is coming."

The combined group drove off two Fierce Ones who threatened. "You give the Wolf People strength," Breaker declared.

Kinder nodded, then asked something he feared to ask. "How many are the Fierce Ones?"

Breaker shook his head, for there were many.

Another man responded, "We have heard of two large groups. If they join together, we will have no chance. We are hoping one group will pass through the land. But even one group will be too large to fight, and we need a way for winning."

"Why has the Summoner called for us to fight, if our chances are slim?" asked Kinder.

Breaker had no answer.

The Wolf People reached a hill topped by rocks and a great cave and found a hundred more persons gathered with some twenty wolves. Among them, were some New Ones among them. This was the most people that Kinder and Huntress had seen together, and among them must be the Summoner.

"There is both fight and fear here," observed Huntress.

Word spread that the two *New Ones*, who had killed Fierce Ones, had come. They came across Flint, his face scarred with loss. His people were now half in number. "If we had known that the man named Kinder was also a New One with power, we would not have–"

"Do not worry," interrupted Huntress. "We are *New Ones*, but I am a Wolf person too. Tell us what happened."

"The Fierce Ones surprised us and killed many of us."

"How many?" asked Kinder.

"Fifty, only half of a greater band. If the full number comes, even with all our wolves...."

Kinder spoke. "I will ask the Summoner why he has gathered us against such odds."

"Let me come with you," said Huntress.

They found him sitting in the cave's mouth. A cool wind stirred from the cave's deeper parts, and Kinder suddenly remembered the place from his wanderings.

The man was sitting in an alcove, his face shrouded.

Kinder called: "One Who Summons, we are the two who just fought the Fierce Ones. We are not great hunters or warriors. Why have you called us to fight so many Fierce Ones?"

The man spoke, his face still turned toward the darkness. "I have heard that her bones are here."

Huntress recognized Sharpener's voice. "You are the one who summons?" she asked. "You have survived!"

"Yes," said Sharpener, and he accepted her hug. "We must fight the Fierce Ones now or later. The world must change from their way. They have strength and numbers that will only grow unless we fight. We cannot leave this land. There is hope here."

"But they are too many," said Kinder. "Why summon us against such odds?"

"She is here. The stories are true...."

Huntress and Kinder were baffled. "Of whom do you speak?"

"You have heard the story of Lion's Mouth. Surely you know."

A flash of memory came to Kinder. "Our mother's body was placed in the cave named Lion's Mouth."

Sharpener turned toward the light, and they saw fresh wounds on his face and chest. Someone had challenged him on the decision to summon, but he had fought and won.

"New Ones placed Bough here after she fought the lion."

Huntress became alarmed. "How do you know such things? Are you one who sees?"

"Who are you?" asked Kinder, his anger rising.

"I am your father," said Sharpener.

"Father?" said Kinder, and he knew.

Sharpener embraced him and said, "I am not your only father, though. I have heard you are a Child of the Elements."

"It is too much," said Kinder, and it took him time to find words. "Yes, I can make the rain and storm come. But how can that stop the Fierce Ones? We must flee."

Sharpener sat back down. "I have spoken to Bough. She has said we must fight from this hill, where there are powers. She was the one who told me to summon."

"How can that be that you heard?" asked Kinder.

"I do not know. I don't have gifts other than to sharpen a stick, to fight, and wander. Yet, when I slept in Lion's Mouth, I heard her."

"Did she say more?" asked Huntress.

"No. But maybe she will speak more to you. Are you not both persons of *Power*? Or so I have heard. And is she not your mother?"

"We have not done such things," Huntress responded. "And is there not a danger in calling the dead?"

"I cannot say if that is so, but I have heard her. She said to fight here, but has not told us how to defeat them. Our hope is with the wolves, and for *New Ones* to show us a way. I heard of deaths of the *Fierce Ones* by *New Ones*. I did not know that I would be summoning Bough's son and her daughter, who was saved from the Hill of Offerings. Maybe she will speak more to her children."

"We don't have the gift," said Kinder.

"Maybe the gift will come to us," said Huntress. "Tomorrow, let us go deeper into Lion's Mouth."

The cave's first chamber was dark, yet light reached the glistening white rocks which hung from the ceiling. Human bones and bear skulls lay near a back wall. On a slab of rock in the center of the chamber, a lion's skull had been placed.

"This is where she spoke," said Sharpener. "We will wait here."

They waited into the night. At one point, they heard steps and sounds. Giving Flower had found them and sat next to Huntress.

Sharpener spoke when he woke in the middle of the night. "Her spirit is quiet tonight."

"Wait!" said Huntress.

Giving Flower's mouth was moving, although no words were coming out. The Sharpener motioned for silence.

They felt a presence, something moving.

"Her spirit is here," said Huntress. It did not speak directly to Huntress or Kinder. Rather, the Trembling One spoke through Giving Flower. "Mother, baby," were the words they heard from her.

"Did she speak to you?" asked Flint when they emerged in the morning.

Huntress told what happened and Flint wondered, "Why does the spirit speak to one who knows so few words?"

"I do not know," said Sharpener. "But it is the way with spirits, to be not easily understood."

One more message came from Bough the next morning, when the Wolf People and the New Ones awoke in the mouth of the cave.

Huntress exclaimed, "I saw Bough in my dream! She was dressed in white skins, and she spoke to me!"

"Did she tell us what to do?" asked Kinder.

"She said, 'Have the heart of a lion, and do not fear death.'"

CHAPTER XIII

Battle Against the Fierce Ones

"What will I say? What can we plan?" Kinder asked Huntress. "The words will come to you. You will know," she answered.

Some hundred and twenty-five strong were gathered around the Lion's Mouth, and Kinder stood before them. His voice boomed, echoing from the cave's mouth.

"I am Son of the Trembling One, the mother who fought a lion and is buried here. I am Howler, who grew up facing wild animals. I am a Child of the Elements and can summon wind and rain, thunder and fire. I am Kinder because I cared for my sister and passed through Hyena Land to find her."

The people murmured, speaking of the one with many names.

"You are also a New One who has killed Fierce Ones," added Breaker. "You will show us how to fight them."

"There are some things we can do," answered Kinder. "We will gather rocks to throw. We will sharpen sticks and learn to throw them. We must stay close together and use our wolves well." Kinder sensed that all this would not be enough, but he did not know what more to say. Throwing spears would do most to even the odds. But it takes time to learn to throw, and a sharpened stick would need a good throw to kill a Fierce One.

Huntress revealed. "Bough has spoken from the Lion's Mouth. She has said not to fear, and to have a lion's heart."

Kinder searched deep for words. "You call yourselves Wolf People or New Ones, but this day we must fight like hyenas. For those who do not throw, we will move as one and hold our sticks as one. Let the Fierce Ones come, but do not let them break our line."

"We need more sharp sticks," Sharpener added.

The Wolf people started working, gathering stones and fashioning spears. Huntress and Kinder began teaching how to throw. "It is better to lose a spear that wounds or kills," they taught, "than to die holding a stick."

The next morning, a young bear surprised the group when it emerged from the cave. Noise had awakened the bear from his sleep. Kinder befriended the bear and fed him. Then the bear laid in the cave's mouth and watched the Wolf People.

"There are scars on this bear's chest," Kinder noted. "Scarred Chest will fight for us like he has fought in the wild."

The Wolf People were amazed at Kinder's way with the bear. "He is a Bear-man too," they declared.

A report came from late arriving Wolf People. A large band of Fierce Ones were heading their way. There was a second, even larger band, but they did not know their whereabouts. Maybe the second group had left or was still wandering about the land.

Kinder surveyed the rocky top of the hill and saw that the men could defend the tall rocks for a time. They could hurl stones and throw spears down the hill.

A flatter way to one side led up to the Lion's Mouth. The Fierce Ones could come this way, Kinder realized, although they had no fear of climbing rocks. Kinder placed the best men and the wolves there. The older people and Huntress, who was with Child, would stay inside the cave. The bear, Scarred Chest, who was slow from waking, would stay to defend them.

Huntress moaned. The stress had made the baby want to come. Kinder ordered a place of birthing to be prepared deeper in the cave. An older woman and Giving Flower would stay with her.

Kinder decided it was time to call upon the Powers. He did not know how they would help, but he would call on them. Holding his hands high, he cried, "Rain and wind, storm and fire! Help us fight the Fierce Ones! We will not survive unless you come!"

Kinder felt no power. Still he added, "Protect Huntress and the child she bears. At least, do not let them die!"

He felt no response and angered, raising his fist. "Would you let the Fierce Ones take us all? You will fight for us! You will protect my woman and her child!"

The Fierce Ones came the next day when the sun was overhead. They were at least eighty, and the Wolf People feared.

Kinder spoke, trying to bring hope. "We have twenty wolves, and each wolf is worth a Fierce One. We can win!" He said this half-believing, for a Fierce One was worth two or three of theirs. "If a hunter uses his spear, the odds are better," he declared.

So the Fierce Ones came from all sides, with no plan but to attack and kill.

A few went up the rocky side, but stones were hurled and the Fierce Ones could not shrug off all the blows. They drew back and came up the flatter way where the other Fierce Ones had gathered.

Here, Kinder and Sharpener led the men, with Flint, Breaker, and other great hunters. There was also the man who stuttered and liked Giving Flower.

Kinder did not know what else they could do. They would have to fight as one and kill. Yet, there were so many against them....

Huntress had not gone into the cave.

"I cannot hide ... My belly aches, but my arm is well enough to throw. I can kill a Fierce One!"

"No. You are ready to birth," said Kinder. "But it was not a firm no. If their defense did not hold, she would not live. And a single dead Fierce One was worth much. She could retreat to the cave when the danger became too great.

"Stay by me," said Sharpener.

The first wave came. Just before the Fierce Ones crashed against them, the Wolf People and New Ones threw sticks, piercing many. The Fierce Ones drew back, howling, pulling sticks from their bodies and breaking them.

The second time, the Wolf People loosed their wolves. Many Fierce Ones were killed and wounded, but wolves died too.

Clouds had gathered, and rain was coming, as it would in the late afternoon. After the Fierce Ones pulled aside bodies, the Wolf People readied for a third wave. *This will be the test,* thought Kinder.

Although there was no rain yet, Kinder announced, "The Elements have been summoned. We will fight in a storm, and we will win!"

The wave of Fierce Ones almost broke through on the third try, but the line of Wolf People and New Ones held their sticks as if one.

One large Fierce One broke through the line. Sharpener saw the danger and arrived in time. When they met, Sharpener's stick smashed against his great arm, and the Fierce One drew back.

Three times Sharpener's stick was grabbed and broken, yet he had another that he pulled up. *Sharpener is a great warrior,* Kinder realized, *yet he never spoke of this.*

The Wolf People fought bravely. Many were left wounded and dying. Huntress had left the line to help them. She had badly wounded a Fierce One with a throw. Exhausted, for the Child was coming, she retreated into the cave to lie down.

The Fierce Ones came a fourth time. The sky was dark, but it was not raining. More on their side were dying; there were wounded all around. The line just held, and the Fierce Ones drew back.

Death faced them on the next assault, and Kinder searched for a final plan. They would retreat to the cave for their last stand. They could hold them off there for one more time. Maybe Scarred Chest would kill many, and the Fierce Ones would be deterred. Yet, even as Kinder thought this, word came from the ones who guarded the rocks at the high places. The large second band of Fierce Ones was coming, and they were not far away.

All hope is lost, Kinder realized. It was now a question of who could get away and escape.

Kinder spoke. "Some must flee if any are to live. We have killed many Fierce Ones, but we cannot win when the second group comes. A few must escape so that our group will live. Others will fight and delay the Fierce Ones. I will lead the ones who stay behind."

The Wolf People hesitated. Sharpener, who was wounded, came forward. "Kinder is right. The ones, who are not wounded, must flee. I will stay and fight."

"Flint will lead the ones who go," ordered Kinder.

Flint protested. "I will stay and fight."

"Someone must lead the ones who flee," the Sharpener countered. "The *New Ones* must survive for another day. Go with them!"

Breaker, who had wounds, nodded. So Flint agreed. The man with the stutter asked about Giving Flower, and Kinder nodded. There was no reason that she must stay and die.

Kinder went into the cave and found Huntress, who had pain and fear in her face. "The baby wants to come, yet won't," she cried.

Kinder's anguish grew. How could he protect his woman and child?

"Giving Flower, come with me!" he ordered, but she grabbed onto Huntress instead.

"Then stay hidden in the cave," Kinder advised, "And do not make any noise."

The thought came that he should kill Giving Flower, for he could not trust her to remain silent. But he could not do that to one who had become part of his family.

When Kinder stepped out of the cave, it was raining lightly. His anger grew at the

Elements, but there was no time for protest. The second group of Fierce Ones had reached the base of the hill and were running upwards.

CHAPTER XIV

Child of Blood

The first group of Fierce Ones sensed victory, that they would kill the last of the Wolf People. Fewer men ringed the cave's mouth, although a bear had been drawn into the fight.

The remaining defenders fought fiercely and called upon the name of Lion Mouth. Yet one by one their sticks were grabbed, and they took blows which left them wounded and dying. The Wolf People would have been overtaken sooner, but the bear fought fiercely.

The fighting paused and Kinder cried, "Go deeper into the cave!" The ones remaining withdrew to a second chamber, which had a narrow entrance.

Only a few made it back, and Kinder saw that Sharpener was not among them. He had gone out into the midst of the Fierce Ones to delay them. They encircled him, and the battle that followed was quick. Sharpener drew a wound, but their champion felled him, and he cried his last.

Thunder rolled. A storm was coming, but it was too late. Kinder raised his stick and struck the cave's wall. "I asked for protection, but we are dying! Would the Powers of the Sky let all the Wolf People and the *New Ones* die? If you must, take me, but let Huntress and my child live!"

Kinder howled.

A sharp crack of thunder sounded. The Fierce Ones looked at the sky. They did not like storms, but they were close to victory. They came on.

Kinder rallied the men at the entrance to the second chamber.

The fighting was fierce against the last of the Wolf People. Then there was only Breaker by his side. He saw Huntress a little further in. She tried to lift herself up, but could not, for the pain of birthing was upon her.

Kinder and Breaker fought fiercely in the narrow entrance where only one could enter.

Lightning lit up the cave's mouth and thunder echoed sharply.

A commotion ensued. The second group of Fierce Ones had arrived, and the first group held off their attack.

Kinder knew that luck, if you could call it luck, had delayed their death. He tended to Huntress, who was heaving in the travail of birth.

Kinder had failed to protect the ones he loved, and the Elements had failed him. Yet others had escaped and would live. *Weren't there many New Ones among them?*

Kinder called to Bough, "We will die here and our bones will be together. We have shown courage!"

Yet more commotion echoed from outside the cave. It was not from the Wolf People, nor from the Elements. Shouting and slamming, the two groups of Fierce Ones were fighting among themselves. Was it for the spoils? Had they imagined there were many women in the cave? They were not able to stop, and the groups of Fierce Ones began fighting each other to the death.

As the Fierce Ones fought, they did not think about the remaining defenders.

"Leave now and take Giving Flower," Kinder told Breaker.

Giving Flower gripped Kinder. She would not leave her father and mother.

"Come with us," said Breaker to Kinder. "Leave the women and children here. You can have a new woman. You will die if you stay with them."

Kinder looked at Huntress, and she whispered, "Go."

He knew that he should listen to her, for he could live for another day. Then he thought of Bough, who would not let go of her early child, when she was fighting wolves, lions, or men.

"I cannot," said Kinder, and he turned to Breaker. "Leave me with the bear."

Breaker wondered. "You have helped us survive. How can you and your woman possibly live?"

Kinder looked up into the sky. "I must stay."

Huntress screamed. The child was coming.

Breaker left. Kinder knew he would tell his story. This was his place to die, like his mother before him.

A boy child emerged, crying. Kinder held his child, an early child. He set him in Huntress arms, and she smiled. With a sharp stone, he cut the cord. Giving Flower was smiling too, and she reached out and touched the child.

They were safe for only a while as the battle raged outside. Rain lashed the cave's mouth, and some wet touched them. The baby cried.

Suddenly, the battle was over. Many Fierce Ones had died, but there were still a dozen from the second group.

The remaining Fierce Ones approached the cave to find and kill the survivors. Kinder saw death and looked upon his child for the last time. There was something he must do that he didn't want to. He took Giving Flower deeper into the cave and struck her, knocking her out.

Then Kinder came out of the cave. He would face the two dozen alone.

Other than to use words, Kinder had no plan. He knew the Fierce Ones did not really talk; yet there were Half-ones among them––it seemed at least two. The sky was darkening, and lightning traced the distant clouds, but neither rain nor storm would save him now.

The Fierce Ones were curious about the one who rose to challenge so many, and they closed around him. When two moved closer to attack, one of the Half-ones raised his hand.

"Let me fight for my life," Kinder demanded. "I will fight any among you. If I take his life, let me and the survivors of my people live. If I lose, then all our lives are forfeit."

Although they knew of such customs, the Half-ones did not give them weight. "Kill him," the second Half-one said. "Then go into the cave and kill all who hide."

Kinder shouted, "I am a Child of the Elements! Let me fight, or the Elements will become angry."

The first Half-one held some superstition. The thunder had become more constant and lightning was dancing across the sky. "Let the fight happen," he said. "We will not lose. Let us see how this New One fights."

The second Half-one nodded. "A large Fierce One cannot lose. And if he fells him somehow, he can be killed anyway."

The Half-ones signaled their champion to come forward. As if on cue, the rain fell harder.

The Fierce One was one-and-a-half times Kinder's size, and even with a stick there would be little hope. When Kinder's stick struck the Fierce One's arm, it seemed to have little effect. Kinder could only keep stepping back, avoiding lunges and buffets. The Fierce One laughed.

The champion almost wrested Kinder's stick away. Then, with one hand holding the stick, the Fierce One struck a blow with his other hand, hitting Kinder's old wounded arm. Pain shot up his shoulder, and now he could only raise it so far. Still, he managed to pull the stick away, for it was wet.

At that point, lightning flashed and thunder clapped nearby. Kinder raised his good arm and called out to the Elements. Nothing stopped the Fierce One from pressing him, striking his stick repeatedly, causing his arms to vibrate with pain.

There was only one thing left to do, something Sharpener had once shown him. "If you are weakening, you can take the life of one who is much stronger. But you must be willing to die...."

Kinder could give a blow that would leave him exposed. If he killed the Fierce One's champion, there was some hope they would just kill him and let Huntress and his baby live. It was all he could think to do.

Yet, he wanted to live with Huntress and his child. In anger he called upon the Elements again. It did not stop the Fierce One, with rock in hand, to deliver a blow that grazed his head. Salty blood burned in one eye. Kinder must act soon, but there was no opening to make his move, and he was weakening. The sky lit again, and thunder even more quickly followed. The Fierce One glanced away. Kinder rolled under the man and struck from underneath. The champion howled and fell. In falling he directed a blow to Kinder's head, and so both died.

The two Half-ones were surprised. "The last of their warriors have died," said the first Half-one. "Yet, he has killed our champion."

The second said, "Let us search the cave and see what is ours. What are words?"

"Maybe we should let one go...." said the first.

The Fierce Ones found Huntress within the cave's mouth, with the remains of birthing on her. They drug her outside, the newborn in her hands.

"She has just birthed," said the first Half-one. "Let her go."

"No, let us kill her," said the other.

Lightning struck over the hill and thunder sounded almost immediately. Rain lashed and wetted them.

The first Half-one looked up. "Do you not have any fear? Did not the warrior who died say that he was a *Child of the Elements*? Did he not say if he killed our champion that the others should live? We should at least let one live."

The other Half-one took a stick and thrust it into Huntress. She gasped, her eyes opened wide. The mother fell with the baby still held in her embrace.

"Enough!" cried the first Half-one.

"There is one left...."

"No! Leave one to the Elements. He will die without his mother."

"No, he will die from my hand," said the second.

A lightning bolt struck a tree within sight, and the smell of burning filled the air.

"Leave a child and one day he rises," cried the Half-one who had killed Huntress. "We must kill the newborn too."

"No, let the child die from the Elements," the other repeated.

"Do you fear a storm like these Fierce Ones?"

"Kill it then," said the other, and he summoned the remaining Fierce Ones to leave.

The Half-one moved to kill the child, but a clean, white streak of lightning felled him, killing him instantly.

The other Half-one hurried away with the departing Fierce Ones.

A crying newborn was left before the cave called Lion's Mouth. It was raining, and the baby lay in the blood of its mother.

The rain stopped, but the newborn was exposed.

There was silence as the sun came out, and a rainbow crossed the sky.

CHAPTER XV

Giving Flower

Then out of the cave wandered Giving Flower. She came upon her mother and shook her, trying to wake her. Then, sobbing, she picked up the newborn and held him close.

The Wolf remnant had not traveled far when they were greeted by Breaker. He reported that the Fierce Ones had fought each other, and that many had died during a great storm. There was hope that some had survived in the cave.

Flint did not want to go back, for he had promised to keep this group safe. Yet if some still lived.... "Four men will come with me and see what has happened," he decided.

When they reached the hill, the sight of so many bodies of Fierce Ones amazed them.

Then, they came across the body of Kinder.

"He fought to the end and killed this great one," discerned Breaker. "He was a great warrior."

They found Huntress pierced through, and the Wolf people marveled that she faced the Fierce Ones even though she had just birthed.

Then they saw the blackened body of a Half-one.

"The Child of the Elements fought back," declared Flint. "He was a Man of Power!"

` An echoing cry from within the cave surprised them. The Wolf People went inside and discovered Giving Flower nursing a baby.

"Yet, two live!" Flint announced. All were amazed that Giving Flower and a baby had survived.

When one of the Wolf People tried to pull the baby away, Giving Flower held tight. She had become fierce with the will of a mother. "My child!" she cried.

The man drew back, and Flint laughed. "Do you not see the mother?"

"She is simple and knows few words," said the man. "You would let her be mother to a Child of Power?"

Flint had grown since he had become leader, and words rose in him. "I do not know much about the ways of Powers, but they are like a storm. Who can predict when one is coming, and how strong it will be? Who would change what the Elements have decided? The Elements have left this child to her. Maybe you would change what the Elements have decided and become like this blackened man?"

The man had no words to answer this.

However, another man said, "A Simple One without a man to father the child cannot care for a child. If the Elements protected her, then leave her and the baby with the Elements."

Flint became angry at the old ways. "Has not this baby already come from the Elements?" Yet, he saw that others feared with all this death about, and some believed it would be better to leave these two behind.

Then one of the Wolf People came forward and spoke in clear words. "I will be her protector." The man who stuttered had spoken with clear words. "I will father this Child of Power."

Flint did not take long to speak. "It is decided. Let them live and be with us."

Others in the group repeated it.

"We have two more things to do yet," said Flint. "The bodies of this child's parents must be placed near their mother Bough, who died here many years ago. Then we must care for the rest of our dead."

They gathered the bodies of Huntress and Kinder and put them on the slab in the cave.

Flint knew that more words were needed, but what could he say? There was so much death all around. Only an infant and a Simple One had survived of those who had stayed. It did not seem like much. He stood still, but found no words.

Then Giving Flower opened her mouth and spoke, "I hear her voice." Her words came out like a song:

> *Kinder and Huntress walk with me*
> *Where light dances in flower land*

"Can what she says be true?" they asked among themselves. How could they argue, when one who hardly speaks made such words? "It must be the Powers speaking through her."

"It's time to go," said Flint. "There are still Fierce Ones about. If we stay together, we will survive. We have a Child of Power among us now. Let us take good care of him, for he is child of us all."

YEARS PASSED AND THE bones of the Fierce Ones still littered Lion's Mouth. The story was told and retold of how Kinder, Huntress, and the Wolf People fought against so many Fierce Ones. It included the birth of a Child of Blood with great power, and what the Elements did that day. Giving Flower too had her part, the one who spoke to the spirits in Lion's Mouth and became a mother.

After this new Child of the Elements was born, a way changed among the Wolf People. They cared for children who were born early, and so more *New Ones* came into the world. In time, the Fierce Ones died away, and the *New Ones* became plentiful, to become the future.

When it stormed, the *New Ones* would remember Kinder, the Child of the Elements. And when they saw rainbows, they remembered their mothers too, Bough and Huntress.

The End

Don't miss out!

Visit the website below and you can sign up to receive emails whenever Michael A. Susko publishes a new book. There's no charge and no obligation.

https://books2read.com/r/B-A-GJLJ-LVQCB

BOOKS2READ

Connecting independent readers to independent writers.

Did you love *Child of the Elements*? Then you should read *The Firekeeper & Spirit of the Long Night*[1] by Michael A. Susko!

In the early Pleistocene era, when fire was invented, a young Firekeeper tends the night fire for the kin. He has a personal intimacy with Fire, with whom he speaks, a being both crafty and true. Two challenges present: he must battle the spirits of the night, and he falls into an impossible love with a woman of the day. Read this book to inhabit the little known stories of our deep history, and to see how human weakness and spiritual strength combine to make us human.

Read more at https://www.allroneofus.com/.

---

1. https://books2read.com/u/bpERnX

2. https://books2read.com/u/bpERnX

Also by Michael A. Susko

A Couple Through Time
Down Below and the Archon's Castle
Up Above and the Runaway
Across the Gulf and Journey Into Un-Time
On the Bay and a Child Found
Down New River & Another World
In the Wild and Do One Wild Thing
On the Mountain and Two Are Missing
To the Beginning and Journey Through Here

Archetypal Worlds
Giant Under the Mountain
The Alien's Gift
The Gold People
Spider Woman and the Timeroc
Darkwood and Dual with the Shadow Side
Quill Ears & the Other Earth
Alwon in Another World: An Archetypal Voyage
Line In the Wall

Biographic Book of Tens
Ten Discoveries from Biology to Spirituality: Hidden & Life-Giving
Connections
Ten Times We Almost Died
Ten Sayings to Guide Our Lives
Ten Mystery Photos: Personal & Cosmological Reflections
Ten Mementos on Our Desk: Remembering Moments
Ten Metadiscoveries We Have Made

Haikus and Photos
Flowers and Haikus
Haikus and Photos: Guatemalan Highlands
Haikus and Photos: Water Birds and Reflections
Haikus and Photos: Seasons of New River
Haikus and Photos: Yosemite Wilderness
Haikus and Photos: California Coast
Haikus and Photos: Canadian Rockies
Haikus and Photos: Hawaii's Exotic Landscapes
Haikus and Photos: Vienna: People, Buildings and Art
Haikus and Photos: Slovakian Castles and Hamlets
Haikus and Photos: Berlin, Light and Dark
Haikus and Photos: New Orleans, City of Immigrants
Haikus and Photos: Antietam Wind and Spirits
Haikus & Photos: Plant Abstractions
Haikus and Photos: Appalachian Beauty
Haikus and Photos: Urban Farm in Sandtown
Haikus and Photos: New York Heights and Ground
Haikus & Photos: Santa Fe Fractal-Pueblo Spirtuality
Haikus and Photos: Monticello's Double Vision

Haikus and Photos: Skeletal Human and Mississippian Art
Haikus and Photos: Mystery Stone's Animal Forms
Haikus and Photos: Plant Forms and Mystery Stone

Stone Formation at Penn Bluff
Haikus and Photos: Presence at Penn Bluff
Haikus & Photos: Mystery Forms at Penn Bluff
Haikus and Photos: Essences at Penn Bluff
Haikus and Photos: World Archetypes at Penn Bluff

The Dreaming Series
Sleek Back & Salamander Dreaming
Streak and Cave Bear Dreaming
Moby and Marsupial Mole Dreaming

The Dream World Trilogy
Delphi, the Time Thief, and the Dream World
Detinna and the Cave God
The Resistance & the Empire

Transformational Stories
Caseness and Narrative: Contrasting Approaches to People
Psychiatrically Labeled
Transformative Experiences, Psychiatric Research, and Informed
Consent
Transformational Stories: Voices for True Healing in Mental Health

Writings from Street People
Street Images
Street Images II

Standalone
Little People & the Time-Rider
Animal Spell
Child of the Elements
The Firekeeper & Spirit of the Long Night
Up Above and Down Below
Life's Dynamic Vulnerability: A Paradigm Shift in Biology
Alien Ally
The Generation of Life: Imagery, Ritual and Experiences in Deep
Caves
Twelve Suspects
2084: Clash of Cults
Bats in the Future
Guard of the Dead
The Imagination Being
Ten Traits of Empire That Every Person Should Know
Aging and Renewal: Living the Full Life
The Meaning, Beauty & Mystery of Dreams: Seven Guidelines and
Seven Tools for Listening
The Fragility of Evolution: A Novel View
Ways We May Be Surprised by Heaven
Why Go Slow When You Can Hurl to Your Destruction!
Haikus & Art: Anima
Stages of the Human Life Cycle: A Novel Logarithmic Perspective
Fifteen Amazing Things About the Body

Watch for more at https://www.allroneofus.com/.

About the Author

The author has lectured on the symbolism of the Paleolithic era and Indigenous cultures worldwide. He has published in evolutionary biology, elaborating a theory which on the survival of the fragile. With humans, children were born increasingly immature, which demanded protection from parents, groups, and spiritual sources of power. In this work, the author imagines the drama in which "early children" come of age.

Read more at https://www.allroneofus.com/.

About the Publisher

AllrOneofUs Publishing seeks out work which will make a novel and qualitative addition to the world literature, and one that will last across generations. Many of these persons are in the later part of their life and have made exemplary contributions which are unrecognized. To cite a few examples, we recommend Rich Mullin's *Ethics and the Full-breasted Richness of Life*, John Susko's *Flowers of the Night: Musings from a Sentimental Son,* and Dr. Curtis Adams' *Psychosis and the Humpty Dumpty Story.*